FOR TH
MONEY

TREVOR ROFF

Scripture Union
130 City Road, London EC1V 2NJ.

By the same author
Wood Enders

© Trevor Roff 1991
First published 1991

ISBN 0 86201 613 4

Phototypeset by Intype, London
Printed by and bound in Great Britain by Cox and Wyman
Ltd, Reading

With grateful thanks to Beryl and Mary for their help in preparing this and previous manuscripts.

This book is dedicated to Mollie, Tim and Merrielle and the many others who made my beach mission days such happy ones.

Contents

~ *1* ~

Wednesday, 25th July

Clouds flitted across the moon as a battered Ford Escort laboured up the rutted track towards the farmhouse. It stuttered and stalled some metres from its destination and ground to an ungainly halt. The silence was punctuated by the whirring of the starter motor as its owner tried unsuccessfully to restart the engine. The car door opened and the young owner leapt out, slamming the door in disgust. The tall youth, only just out of his teens, picked his way gingerly along the rock-strewn roadway, zipping up his anorak against the cool evening chill. The moonlight revealed a dark-haired man, tight-lipped and with a secretive air. Only the darting eyes betrayed the fear of someone unused to such cloak-and-dagger stuff. After all, he reasoned, why all these precautions about having a meeting place miles from anywhere? Why not meet in the town itself, like normal people do?

He cursed under his breath as his foot slipped on a loose stone and his trainer splashed into a puddle. Clearly he was not in a good mood. He looked up and seemed relieved to see the black outline of the derelict farmhouse which now loomed above him. The fence had long ago rotted and fallen down, leaving just the gate-posts drunkenly standing guard, but he still fumbled at the gate latch before walking quickly up the even garden path. Stupid, really, he thought to himself, as he approached the doorless front entrance.

Nervously he crossed the threshold into the cavernous blackness. 'Hello,' he called in a wimpish voice, then coughed angrily to himself and called again in what he hoped was a more confident tone. 'Anyone there?'

He listened as the sound of his own voice died away. Suddenly a harsh chuckle sounded in his left ear. 'You sound like you're gonna wet yourself any minute. Come on in and stop messing about. You've kept me waiting long enough.'

'Sorry, Baz,' he said. 'This is a pig of a place to find and then my car was playing up. It keeps stalling.'

'Yeah, I know, I heard you, same as anyone for half a mile around would've. Do you have to announce your arrival to the whole world?'

'Well I don't know why you had to arrange to meet in this God-forsaken place. What's wrong with the pub?'

'I told you, Nick, it's more private. Now come over here so we can stop shouting at each other. You never know who might be walking about.'

Nick followed the sound of Baz's voice and promptly hit his head on the lintel. 'Ouch!' he gasped as Baz's raucous chuckle hit him for the second time that evening. 'Can't you shine a light or something?'

'Should've brought your own, shouldn't you?' laughed Baz, as he switched on his torch and pointed it at the floor. 'Sit down over here before you do any more damage.'

Nick looked around for a clean place to sit amongst the old cans, newspapers and layers of dust. The fireplace looked the safest bet so he eased himself down against the mantelpiece and turned to look at Baz. The torchlight

gave a ghostly appearance to the thick-set features Nick
had come to know well during the past few months.
With his scrawny black hair, ready wit and outlandish,
extrovert appearance, Baz never went unnoticed. At
twenty-five he already had a definite beer paunch and
his twisted foot prevented him joining in any sporting
activities, but his wicked sense of fun usually made him
the centre of attention and very popular. He was a mean
hand at darts too, and Nick always smiled at the memory
of the time when Baz deliberately missed the dartboard at
their local and cracked the glass in the landlord's favourite
picture of the Queen Mum. How he got away with his
cheek to the irate landlord, Nick never knew. But survive
he did and came out on top too, it seemed, most of the
time. Why Baz had singled him out for special favour
Nick did not understand, unless it was because Nick
never refused to pay for Baz's drinks. That was often,
Baz being unemployed. Maybe I'm just too soft in the
head, Nick mused to himself. Must be, I suppose, to
come out here tonight, like he told me. I don't know
what I'm doing here.

As if Baz had heard his unspoken comment, he broke
the silence. 'Well, aren't you going to ask me what we're
doing here, mate?'

'You said something about a job last week, but it must
be something special to keep you from your booze,' said
Nick, pointedly.

'Yeah, it is, which is why I'm not discussing it with
too many flapping ears around. Much quieter here, more
peaceful like. No one comes prying around – that's why
I like it. Even keep some of my things here, things I
don't want others to know about.' Baz shone his torch
over to the far corner, where Nick could make out some
cardboard boxes and a sleeping bag.

'You don't sleep here, surely?' laughed Nick.

'Nah, I got a home to go to, same as everyone else,

that is when me dad doesn't get drunk and throw me out. But when Sandra and me wanna be by ourselves – know what I mean –' and Baz gave Nick a knowing wink.

'Oh yeah!' Nick grinned back, not wanting to appear shocked. 'What's in all them cardboard boxes?' he said, changing the subject.

'Mind your own business!' snapped Baz. 'You don't need to worry your little head over them, so don't get nosy!'

Nick said nothing but it didn't take a genius to work out that this was where Baz kept his store of stolen goods. After all, wasn't he always boasting how easy it was to find things that had fallen off the back of a lorry, and didn't he always happen to have handy the very watch or camera that someone wanted to buy?

Nick broke the tension. 'Well come on, then. Tell me about this job. What's so special about it?'

'OK. Keep your hair on!' Baz paused for effect. 'How would you like to have a half share of £5000?'

Nick whistled softly. He had expected Baz to propose something shady – but not on this scale.

Baz took Nick's reaction as encouragement and continued. 'All it takes is half an hour's quiet work and we can get our hands on at least five grand, all in used notes and cash. Interested?'

'Yeah. You bet,' enthused Nick, though inside he felt panic rise. Did he really want to get involved in something this big? He'd never had much scruple about the odd bit of thieving from work. It was easy to slip the odd pullover or shirt out the back door of the warehouse where he worked and flog them to his mates. Lots of people did it, anyway. But this was different. He licked his lips nervously as Baz went on.

'You know the council depot in Lincoln Street? Well I happen to know there's a safe inside those offices – a friend of Sandra's works there.'

'So what? Lots of offices have safes in them,' interrupted Nick.

'Listen, will you!' snarled Baz. 'I don't like people butting in when I'm talking, 'specially not smart Alecs like you. Just 'cos you've got a job you think that makes the rest of us thickheads or something!?'

'No, of course not. Calm down. I won't say another word,' said Nick, surprised at this sudden bitterness in Baz's voice. Baz had always laughed off his unemployment before and even boasted of his freedom while others were slaves to their 'capitalist bosses'. Now he had exposed a vulnerability Nick had never suspected.

'Now Sandra and me got talking the other night to this friend of hers, see. Well, it seems this friend, Yvonne, has the job of taking in all the cash every day and counting it. Then she takes it down the bank with an escort like, and pays it in. Now it turns out that this money is the takings from all over Shelham – the car parks, the putting greens, the deckchair hire and the like. It all comes down to little Yvonne in her little office where she counts it all.'

Nick found himself listening to all this with mounting concern and couldn't prevent himself voicing a protest. 'But this is heavy stuff, Baz. It's far too risky to just snatch the money in broad daylight. It'll be armed robbery and assault. It's too risky!'

'Will you shut up and listen!' hissed Baz again. 'Who said anything about armed robbery? The point is they're short-staffed at the office at the moment so Yvonne has to wait for the manager to come with her to the bank. They won't let her go on her own – too many suspicious characters around, like me!' He laughed at his own little joke which Nick had to admit was funny the way Baz told it.

'Now the manager's a very busy man, what with two

other depots in the area and his own office in Cromagh, so he can only go with Yvonne on Mondays and Wednesdays. That means that by Friday afternoon poor little Yvonne is sitting on a nice little pot of money and feeling worried sick that some horrible villain is gonna come bounding in with a mask over his head, do violence to her pretty little body and ride off with the takings.'

Nick was now laughing at the picture Baz presented of the helpless female and the big, bad criminal. He was being carried along by the fun of the way Baz told it and the force of the older man's personality. Baz suddenly became serious again.

'The point is, mate, that that money will be sitting in that nice little office in that nice little safe all over the weekend with no nice little Yvonne to guard it. Just sitting there waiting for anyone who knows it's there to relieve Yvonne of the worry of it on Monday morning.'

'But won't she suspect it's you, then, if the money's stolen over the weekend?' put in Nick.

'Do me a favour! I'm a friend of hers, aren't I? Sandra and her are bosom pals. I told her she'd got nothing to worry about and she believed me. She thinks butter wouldn't melt in my mouth.'

Nick found that easy to believe, knowing Baz's charms.

'And there's another reason why no one will suspect me,' said Baz. 'And that's where you come in.'

'Oh, what's that?' asked Nick, interested in spite of himself at the ingenuity of the plan.

'The only way to get into the depot yard is to climb those gates. The lock and chain would take too long and they'd be a dead giveaway as soon as anyone comes poking around. I've been and checked, so I know. Climbing the gates is the only way.'

Nick began to see the light. Baz with his gammy foot could never climb anything, which explained why Baz needed Nick's help. It would also give Baz a very good alibi.

'Very clever, Baz. You're a genius,' said Nick and he sensed Baz's pleasure at the remark. 'But aren't you forgetting something?'

'What's that?' said Baz, annoyed at this sudden doubt.

'How are you going to get in?'

Baz relaxed again. 'Nothing easier mate. Once you're in, you tie a rope to something and throw it over to me. I might have a spastic foot but I've got muscles here that'll make rope-climbing child's play. Feel that.'

Nick reminded himself with a grin of those noisy arm-wrestling matches in the pub which Baz seemed invariably to win. He couldn't fault Baz's reasoning and with Baz here in the privacy of the torch-lit room, it all seemed so simple and easy. And the money! That was certainly appealing. As Baz talked on, planning all the minor details, Nick again found himself carried along by the thrill and fascination of it all, forgetting the risk and the penalty in the excitement of the challenge. How easy it all seemed and what an adventure! Nick would often look back in the months ahead and remember the feelings he enjoyed that first night.

Much later they emerged from the house into the moonlight to walk back to Nick's car. Nick looked down on the dancing lights of Shelham, five miles below them. A sleepy seaside town, it was a bastion of middle-class respectability and East Anglian character, ten years behind the times and proud of it. It had always been Nick's home, but standing now apart from it, Nick felt himself grow out of its hold on him. He would break free from its shackles and prove that he could be a man in the big outside world. This plan of Baz's was just the break he needed. The summer breeze quickened and Nick heard far off the lilting rhythmic swell of the Norfolk surf and smelled the familiar salt tang. A sudden misgiving overtook him but he shrugged it off as sentimental nonsense.

'One last thing,' said Baz, breaking into Nick's thoughts as they got into the car. 'Get yourself a decent motor for Friday night. I don't want you waking up all of Shelham with your clapped-out engine.'

'It'll be fine when I've fixed the timing, Baz. Honest, it just needs a bit of tuning,' pleaded Nick.

'Don't argue with me. If you're in on this you do things my way, or not at all. Now are you in or aren't you?' Baz demanded.

Nick hesitated only a fraction of a second before nodding his head. 'Yeah, okay. I'll see if I can borrow Dad's Cavalier.'

'Well see you do, then. And don't let me down or I'll make sure it becomes very uncomfortable for you around these parts,' threatened Baz. 'Now I'll meet you as arranged Friday night and don't forget the gear. You can drop me off at the corner. We don't want to be seen together in town and I can walk from here. Had to walk all the way up anyway,' he grinned ruefully. 'I'll soon be fitter than you are.'

'No chance,' Nick grinned back as he let Baz out. Their relationship restored, Nick drove home with a tingling anticipation of the exploits ahead.

~ 2 ~

'That's 51p change, madam. Thank you,' said Jenny, with a practised automatic lilt. After all, when you'd worked in the same High Street chemist's ever since leaving school two years ago, you were entitled to be a little bored with the unchanging daily routine. She breathed an audible sigh of relief.

'And don't you dare show your face in here again!' she added for good measure, almost loud enough for the last customer of the day to hear. A horrified gasp behind her made her turn around sharply.

'You are a caution, Jenny! She might have heard you,' giggled Andrea, the only other junior assistant. Older than Jenny, she had not worked there so long and being a quieter person altogether, was used to playing second fiddle to Jenny's lively personality.

'So what! I'd love to have seen the look on her face if she did hear! As from ten seconds ago, I couldn't care less. Break out the champagne, fling off my uniform, I am no longer the junior employee of Kingston and Sons. Hooray! Freedom at last!' And to emphasise her words Jenny dramatically tore off her assistant's overalls and

13

flung them into Andrea's arms.

Andrea, in another fit of giggles, barely managed to catch the flimsy nylon. 'Until two weeks' time, you mean, when you have to come back from your holiday,' she reminded Jenny.

'Oh, what did you have to go and spoil it for? I was just enjoying my flight of fantasy. What a bore you are, Andrea!'

'Pardon me, I'm sure,' replied Andrea, making a face. She was used to Jenny and didn't let it ruffle her. 'Lucky you, anyway. Two whole weeks away from this place, in the middle of summer, too. I can't have my holidays till September, what with old Mrs Cratchett wanting most of August because of her children being off school. Still, Minorca'll be a bit cheaper then and I can avoid the crowds maybe. Where are you going? Somewhere warm? Greece? Tunisia?'

There was a slight hesitation in Jenny's voice before she casually passed off the question. 'Norfolk, actually.'

'Norfolk?' Andrea sounded incredulous. 'That's the back of beyond, isn't it?'

'No need to sound so superior,' retorted Jenny. 'I'm going with my friend Liz, as a matter of fact. She suggested it and it's going to be a lot of fun.' She said this almost as much to convince herself as Andrea, who fortunately didn't seem to notice.

'What sort of holiday is it, then? Just the two of you going?' said the older girl, genuinely interested.

'Oh no! We're joining a mixed houseparty, all in one huge house. I don't know much about it, but Liz knows someone who's been – she reckons it's great fun.'

'I bet! One large mixed houseparty. Sounds really groovy,' said Andrea, opening her eyes wide in feigned shock. 'But I didn't reckon you for a swinger, Jenny.'

'It's not that at all,' snapped Jenny. 'You've got a dirty mind.'

14

'All right. No need to get prudish. So what do you do?'

'Oh, you know, the usual seaside holiday things,' said Jenny casually, desperately hoping that Andrea would stop probing and showing up her ignorance. After all, she ought to know what sort of a holiday she was going on, didn't she?

'Oh, I know, building sandcastles and donkey rides,' said Andrea sarcastically.

But Jenny would not be drawn further. 'Yes, that's right. Come on, hurry up or Mrs Cratchett will lock us in for the night.'

The two girls quickly packed away and followed the older woman out into the street. They parted company cheerfully enough, with smiling good wishes for Jenny from the other two and promises to write them both a postcard. Then Jenny was left to her own thoughts as she walked the half mile home.

Why did Andrea have to go and spoil her day like that, she thought savagely, just when she was getting ready to celebrate her holidays. Especially when she'd even scrounged tomorrow off too so that she and Liz could travel up in plenty of time for the start on Saturday. But the start of what? Jenny began to realise that the reason Andrea had made her so cross was that she didn't know the answer to her questions. When most normal people would be lapping up the sun in the Mediterranean she had agreed to Liz's plan for them both to spend a fortnight in the wastes of East Anglia, at a place she'd never heard of – what was it? Stedding? Stedham? – 'No, Shelham, that's it,' she said aloud, startling a passer-by.

But doing what? Andrea's questions bounced back at her. Liz had said it was a beach mission, living with twenty or so other people, working with children, games on the beach, barbecues. Liz had described it as fun and said it wouldn't seem like hard work at all, according to her friend. Liz had done most of the paperwork, sending off for details, though Jenny had had to fill in quite a detailed form about herself, and even get Mr Barnes, their minister, to write a reference for her. Oh yes, that was another thing. Jenny knew it was a Christian thing; Liz had told her that too and said that that made it even better, sharing a holiday with lots of other Christians. Jenny wasn't so sure; most of the Christians she knew in her church weren't exactly live wires, especially the boys!

Still, there was no backing out now! And it was her annual summer holiday after all. She determined then and there, that whatever Andrea might be thinking, whatever Liz might do, she was going to get the most out of this holiday. She would really make it hum, even if some dreary Christian wallflowers tried to stop her.

That was Jenny all over. She called it knowing her own mind; being headstrong was how her parents would have described it. They had been disappointed two years ago when Jenny refused to go to sixth form college and instead got herself a job at the local chemist's. Getting out into the world and being independent was Jenny's reason and they knew her too well to try and change her mind once it was made up. If Jenny had any regrets during those two years she certainly didn't let her parents know.

But Jenny didn't change everything when she left school. She still attended Grove Street Baptist with her parents and Liz and seemed settled there with a good crowd of young people. Jenny relied on her Christian friends at Grove Street more than she would have admitted, despite her occasional rude comment about some of them. It had not been that difficult for Liz to persuade her to go on holiday together, and Jenny's main thought in anticipating the next fortnight was that she and Liz would be together. Her parents, too, had encouraged her to join what was obviously a worthwhile cause and had even offered to pay her living expenses – which Jenny had firmly declined. 'Serving the Lord' was how her parents described Jenny's holiday to their friends and while Jenny would never have described it in those terms she was secretly pleased to be in her parents' good books. Makes a change, after all, she thought ruefully, as she opened the front door of their respectable, middle-class semi-detached house.

'Is that you, Jenny?' called out her mother's voice.

'Yes,' she replied, and under her breath, 'Who else would it be?'

'Oh, good. Your supper's nearly ready. Liz has been on the phone. She'd like you to phone her back when you can.'

'Oh, right. I expect she wants to go over the travel details with me again. She knows what a scatterbrain I am for remembering.'

'I am glad you and Liz are going together. She's such a nice girl – and she does succeed in getting you organised, which is what you need,' concluded Mrs Cooke primly.

'Yes, Mother,' Jenny countered, pouring out some tea and knowing her mother hated to be called that.

'Oh, I know you think I go on, Jenny,' said Mrs Cooke, 'but I just want you to know how pleased your father and I are that you're going on this beach mission, giving up your holiday to serve the Lord when you could be off sunbathing in the Mediterranean.'

'Serving the Lord!' There was that phrase again. Jenny couldn't help replying with rather too much feeling, 'Look, Mum, I don't know what grand ideas you have about this thing, but I am certainly not going to give up my holiday, as you put it, in order to be a Sunday School teacher for fourteen days running. Liz and I are going to enjoy ourselves with a lot of other people our age and do what we want to do. After all, I deserve a holiday after all these months at Kingston's, don't I?'

'Yes, of course, dear,' agreed Mrs Cooke, surprised at this outburst and not wanting to provoke her daughter further. She served up their meal without any more comments and the two ate in a strained atmosphere, Mrs Cooke desperately thinking of ways to restore her daughter's good humour and Jenny with her mind full of plans for the fortnight ahead. She excused herself as soon as she could to return Liz's phone call.

Two miles further down the Caterham Road, Liz Allenby was putting the finishing touches to her packing. She was the same age as Jenny and they had been friends throughout their school careers. Neither knew what drew them to each other because they were such opposites in many ways. Jenny was scatty and headstrong, Liz was academic and organised, and often one would get on the other's nerves because of their differences. But what they did share was a love of life and a love for people. Both warm-hearted and outgoing girls, it was natural they should find each other that first day at Whyteleafe High School, and go on to form a friendship that not only withstood all the pressures of teenagehood but was strong enough to reach out and include other girls in need of friendship.

Theirs would be a lasting relationship, Liz felt, and she was disappointed when Jenny decided not to join her in the Whyteleafe Sixth Form. But Liz had no more success than Mr and Mrs Cooke in changing Jenny's mind and Liz too knew Jenny's strong desire for independence. So now they obviously saw less of each other than before, except at church, for by this time Liz had become a baptised member too. It was curiosity which first drew Liz to the church when she discovered that Jenny and her parents regularly attended and her interest in sharing the religious part of her new friend's life gradu-

18

ally became a strong personal desire to know God herself. It was quite an emotional night when Liz finally lowered the barriers in her life and admitted that God was a person who had loved her for a long time.

But it had not been easy. Her family and friends had mostly misunderstood and even scoffed at her new interest in 'religion'. Jenny had been her greatest help in those difficult days and she would always be grateful for the time Jenny had given up to be with her, to encourage and cheer her up. Now it seemed that Jenny was the one in need of a good friend for she seemed restless and unfulfilled, usually moaning about her job and lack of money and finding fault with the way things were done at church and with life in general. Liz longed that Jenny would find life exciting and good again.

'Dad's home! Mum says can you come and help get tea ready,' called Ian, her elder brother. He had followed his father into the building trade and had also inherited his father's chauvinistic attitude towards women. Liz sighed and abandoned her half-full suitcase. She knew there was no point in asking Ian to help Mum and could imagine, too, the sharp words from her mother if she didn't appear soon in the kitchen.

Downstairs she collected the cutlery and laid the table, making sure that her father and brothers had a good view of the television from where they would sit. She knew what grumbles there would be otherwise! She felt grumpy herself inside – after all, it wouldn't hurt Ian or Charlie to lift a finger to help just once, would it? – especially when she had so much to get ready for tomorrow.

'Hurry up, Liz! I need you to strain the potatoes. You know I can't lift the heavy pan with my hands, and can you open the baked beans and put them on?' said her mother, who was standing at the grill, fork in hand.

Sausages again, thought Liz. 'Wouldn't the boys rather

have chips?' she volunteered aloud and immediately regretted it.

'They can lump it,' retorted Mrs Allenby. 'I've run out of ready-prepared ones and I haven't got time to slice them myself. It's a pity you didn't stir yourself to do them if you're so worried about your brothers.'

'I was upstairs packing. You know I'm leaving first thing in the morning,' said Liz, struggling with the can opener.

'Yes, I know you are, more's the pity!' snapped her mother. 'I can't think what possessed you to chuck in that holiday job of yours. Good money it was and they wanted you till the end of August. I think you're a proper little fool.'

'But you know this holiday was booked months ago,' said Liz in what she hoped was her most reasonable and placatory voice; she recognised the warning signs of her mother's rising temper.

'But it's not even a proper holiday,' protested Mrs Allenby. 'Working with kids and trying to make them all religious like you. Waste of time if you ask me!'

'It's what I want to do, Mum,' said Liz quietly.

'You'd have done much better to keep that job through the summer, then have plenty of spending money for a real holiday before you go off to Art College in September,' continued her mother. 'But you always think you know best, ever since you got in with that religious crowd. Too good for your own family now you've become a Christian!'

Liz contented herself with a subdued 'Oh, what's the use!' under her breath. She knew from bitter experience the folly of rising to her mother's bait. It only produced angry words, hasty accusations and further misunderstandings. It was small wonder that she now communicated less and less with her family, but this only increased her alienation from her mother, and produced those angry words from a woman who had tried and failed to understand her own daughter.

The Allenby meal-time was no more of a success than the Cookes' one had been, though Liz's father and brothers were too engrossed in EastEnders to notice any frostiness in the atmosphere. It was with relief that Liz heard the doorbell ring.

'That'll be Jenny,' she said, jumping up from the table. 'Is it all right if I go?'

'What about the washing up? Leaving me to do it all, I suppose,' snapped her mother.

Liz's temper flared. Surely she could be excused that chore, this evening of all evenings. She bit her tongue, hard, before trusting herself to reply. 'Oh, all right. Jenny can help me do it,' Liz heard herself say, then added sarcastically, 'I'm sure she won't mind,' as she hurried to answer Jenny's second ring.

'Hi, Liz, how's things?' said Jenny breezily.

'Come and help me do the washing up, and don't say another word,' warned Liz and led a puzzled Jenny into the kitchen. She cleared the remaining plates off the dining table, then closed the door on the noise of the television and her family. At least then she could have Jenny to herself away from flapping ears.

'Come on. I'll wash and you can wipe,' said Liz, throwing a tea-towel in Jenny's direction and running the hot water. 'What's the matter?' she said, seeing the look on Jenny's face. 'You don't object to a spot of hard work, I suppose.'

'No, of course not,' said Jenny, taken aback. 'It's just I didn't expect you to be having to do this.'

'Why, don't you have to wash up – oh no, I forgot – you've got a dishwasher, haven't you?' retorted Liz with feeling.

'Look, I can go if you'd rather. I can see I've come at a bad time,' said a rather hurt Jenny.

'Oh no, don't do that! I'm sorry, Jenny. It's just that Mum's been getting at me and everything was bottling up inside me. I shouldn't have taken it out on you. Don't feel you've got to wipe up, only I must do this or I'll never hear the end of it from Mum.'

'That's all right,' said Jenny, smiling again. She was never one to bear grudges. Picking up the first plate to dry she blushed inwardly at the memory of her mother single-handedly clearing up the kitchen. 'What's your Mum been saying, then?'

'Keep your voice down,' hushed Liz, glancing worriedly at the door. 'She's been nagging me about going on this beach mission and giving up all the money I would have earned if I'd stayed in that boring old holiday job I had.'

'Oh, not that again!' said Jenny. 'When is she going to realise that it's your life and she's got no right to interfere? You are eighteen, after all, same as me. I wouldn't let my parents tell me anything!'

'No, I know you wouldn't,' smiled Liz. 'But it's not that simple. Be grateful that you've got Christian parents, Jenny. I wish I had.'

'Huh! I don't know that having Christian parents is any better. They still try to tell you what to do in their lovey-dovey "We know best" tone of voice. It makes me sick sometimes.'

'Maybe you're right, Jen, but I'd still swop places with you any day. Anyway, we'll have a fortnight away from all of them. That's something to look forward to,' Liz smiled, recovering her temper. 'Leave the rest to drain and you can come and help me finish packing.'

'Work never stops for you, does it?' laughed Jenny. 'I can't do my packing until Mum's finished ironing my things and Dad gets my case down from the loft – when he gets home from work, that is!'

'What it is to be the idle rich!' mocked Liz. 'You won't

have much time to pack in the morning, though, if we're going to catch the right train.'

'I thought you said we didn't have to arrive at Shelham till the afternoon.'

'That's right, but it's all a question of getting the right connection at Liverpool Street. Come on, I've got the train timetable upstairs. We'll go through it again.' Liz led the way to her bedroom and they spent a happy hour or so planning their journey to a holiday that would hold more than they bargained for.

~ 3 ~

Friday, 27th July

Damian Everet downed his tools at exactly one o'clock and stretched his gangly arms high above his head. At six foot one, he had inherited his father's height and build, but his mother's good looks were evident in his blue eyes and wavy blond hair.

'That's it. Lunchtime,' he announced to everyone in general. 'Who's coming down The Fox then?' he inquired of the three or four other lads engaged in various tasks around the garage where they worked. Most of them either ignored Damian, or smiled and shook their heads. Though they too enjoyed visiting their local pub after work they were either too shy or too careful to go drinking with Damian at lunchtime. There was no telling what Mr Evans, the foreman, might say if he smelt beer on their breath in the afternoon. Two of the lads were on YTS schemes at Hazeley's Garage and needed a good word from old Evans to have a job next year. Besides, no one wanted to feel the rough edge of the old man's tongue, which was as fiery as it was unpredictable. Damian, though, had a devil-may-care attitude towards most things.

'Come on then, Al, it looks like it's just the two of us again,' Damian said to the young man nearest to him. 'We'll leave these little boys to eat their mums' sandwiches in peace.'

Al was Damian's only real friend at Hazeley's. He was shorter and darker than his companion with steady grey eyes that showed a depth of character lacking in most young men. Like Damian he had been offered a YTS place as a trainee mechanic two years ago and they had both performed sufficiently well to be offered a permanent job twelve months later. But while Damian revelled in being under a car bonnet and servicing some of the classy cars that came to Hazeley's, Al hankered after a desk job in the sales department, believing that a suit and tie and a sales commission was the way to the sort of life he wanted to lead.

'Right, Damian. I've had enough of this smell of oil for one morning.'

'Don't knock it, mate. That smell is your bread and butter, don't forget,' Damian reminded him.

'Yeh, I know, but I can't wait till old Snelling in sales decides to sling his hook and I can get a chance there. His retirement's long overdue anyway.'

'Oh, knock it off, Al, I've heard it all before,' joked Damian. 'Forget it and come and have a drink. It's your shout first.'

They finished their wash and scrub-up and strode jauntily out into the hot summer's day for their forty-five minute break. Despite Al's job aspirations he was content to play second fiddle to Damian in their relationship. Damian liked to be the life and soul of the party, always acting the fool and telling more jokes in the garage than most of them could remember. He lived for the moment, spending money as soon as he earned it, so that by Friday lunchtime, Al knew, it would be him buying all the drinks. Al liked a good time too, but had definite goals in life, which Damian lacked. While Damian would probably still be in the same job ten years from now, Al knew where he saw himself – Sales Manager of Hazeley's.

Yet Damian had not many friends apart from Al, and his succession of girlfriends was always short-lived. Al realised that Damian needed him as a friend more than he would ever admit and, after all, Damian was a laugh and they'd had some good times together. All this Damian was unaware of. Despite his loud mouth, he was devoid of cunning and was open and trusting by nature. Being no judge of people he seemed only to attract and be attracted by fair weather friends like Al.

They went into The Fox and Al signalled to Jo, everyone's favourite barmaid. 'Usual then, is it?' he asked.

'Yeah, and a pork pie if you're offering,' said Damian. Al grinned, guessing the state of Damian's finances.

'Go and set up the bar billiards, if you've got enough money for that,' he taunted. The sarcasm was lost on Damian who wasted no time in grabbing the cues before anyone else got in first. Everything's a game to him, smiled Al ruefully to himself.

For the next half-hour they enjoyed the skill and luck of their favourite pub pastime, Damian carried away by the excitement of the scoring, going for big match-winning breaks only to lose them by knocking a skittle down. Al meanwhile played carefully and methodically, building up his smaller, safer breaks into an unassailable lead. Time eventually beat Damian and they spent their last five minutes of freedom relaxing over their half-empty glasses.

'Got any plans for the weekend, then Al?' asked Damian, in a rare moment of concern for his friend.

'Yeah, I thought I might try and find a new suit in town tomorrow. Unwin's have got a sale on.'

'A suit! What on earth for?' said Damian, astonished.

26

'Oh, I know. You're still after that sales job, aren't you? It beats me. They're all a lot of show-offs up in that showroom.'

Al was unruffled. 'You ought to think about your future too, you know, Damian. You should be making plans like I am, know where you want to get to.' Damian snorted into his glass. 'All right, mock if you like. But I bet you're not even looking further than Saturday night, are you?'

'Dead right, mate, only it's Friday night this week. Shirley finishes her holiday tomorrow – going home to boring Birmingham – so tonight's our last night. And a great night it's going to be, if I play my cards right.'

'Very nice too,' smiled Al. He had to admire Damian's success with the girls. Every month or so Damian would have a new one in tow and he seemed to be an expert at finding ones here on holiday, ready and willing for a no-strings holiday fling. Al couldn't help envying him. 'So we can all expect a graphic account tomorrow morning at work, can we?' he added.

'You've got a dirty mind, Alistair, my son,' grinned Damian in the fake Cockney accent he often liked to assume. 'But I'll see if I can give you fellers a few crumbs from my table tomorrow,' he added mockingly.

Al sniggered and elbowed Damian in the ribs just as he swallowed his last mouthful of beer. With a splutter of protest Damian lunged after the laughing retreating figure of his workmate and in high spirits they joked and jostled their way back to work.

At two-thirty that afternoon, two girls, weighed down with two heavy suitcases each, made their way through the crowds at Norwich railway station to the main entrance, where they hoped to be met by someone called Daniel. Liz and Jenny had had a frenetic day so far and were desperately hoping that this final part of their journey at least would be uneventful.

Jenny had been late to begin with, as Liz had feared she might be. She had mislaid her hairdryer and had arrived breathlessly, full of apologies. They had missed their intended train to East Croydon and their connection to Victoria. A hasty dash across London by Underground left them at Liverpool Street station with only minutes to spare and no time to buy tickets. Flinging themselves on the train to Norwich at the last minute, they were both like limp rags. Liz had tried to make light of it and accept Jenny's apology graciously but even her usual even-temperedness was severely stretched. It only needed one more thing to go wrong and she felt she wouldn't be able to hold back the tears. If this Daniel didn't turn up she'd just turn round and go home again, beach mission or no beach mission.

'Don't worry. I'm sure he'll be there,' Jenny reassured her. Liz didn't feel reassured. She found it hard to share Jenny's ability to laugh off misfortune and she couldn't avoid the reflection that none of the misfortune need have happened if Jenny had been on time. That thought was unchristian, she rebuked herself, but it didn't make her feel better.

The entrance to Norwich station was a mass of cars, buses, taxis and people. Both girls looked round in bewilderment until the stream of hurrying people forced them to move out of the main entrance and stand by the front wall. The chances of them spotting their promised lift didn't look too good, thought Liz moodily.

After the departure of the London train five minutes later, however, the crowds had noticeably thinned and a dark-skinned youth in sandals approached them.

'Hi! Are you Liz Allenby and Jenny Cooke?' he smiled at them.

'Yes!' chorused both girls, their relief evident as their faces broke into grateful smiles.

28

'Right! Well, I'm Daniel. I've got my car over here. Hope I haven't kept you waiting.'

'Oh no, not at all,' breezed Jenny, taking the lead in her usual gregarious manner. She lost no time in sizing Daniel up as they made their way to his rather battered 2CV car. With faded jeans and fashionable hair style, he was a definite improvement on some of the teenage boys back home. She eagerly took the front passenger seat for herself and looked forward to their car ride together.

Daniel chatted away happily to them as they bounced and swerved their way to Shelham. This was his second year, he told them. He'd loved every minute of it last year and was looking forward to meeting the team again and some of the children he'd remembered.

'It's quite a family affair, really,' he said. 'Lots of families come year after year for their holidays, and for the beach mission. The kids love it and I suspect the parents love getting their offspring off their hands for a few hours each day. A lot of the team are regulars too,' he added. 'Tim's a great leader – you'll love him – and Kate's coming back to do the cooking again – the food's marvellous.' His relaxed conversation was unwittingly giving the girls a far better recommendation for beach missions than they'd had from the official letters and leaflets, and they were soon quietly excited about the next two weeks.

'Here we are, then!' Daniel said as the car's squeaky brakes announced their arrival outside No. 33 Augustine Street. 'Green Shutters! That's the wonderful name they've given this old house, though the shutters vanished years ago. Leave your bags here and come inside and meet the others.'

Daniel led them into the high ceilinged hall of Green Shutters, where a slim middle-aged man was flicking through a pile of post on the hall table. Looking up at their approach his youthful face broke into a wide grin.

'Daniel! Good to see you!' he beamed, pumping Daniel's hand up and down. 'And you must be Liz and Jenny – now which is which?'

Laughingly the girls introduced themselves and were ushered through into the dining room where they were given a very welcome cup of tea served by Kate. The next two hours were spent in finding the girls' beds in an eight berth dormitory, unpacking, and seemingly endless introductions to various members of the twenty-six strong team. Six o'clock supper found them all ravenously hungry and Kate's cooking did not disappoint them. Her reputation as a good cook was a well-earned one, agreed all the first-timers on the team. At the end of the meal, Tim rose to his feet.

'Well, welcome, everyone! I think I've said hello to just about all of you. It's good to see all the old faces back again and a special welcome to the first-timers.' Liz and Jenny smiled awkwardly as several pairs of eyes sparkled at them and the other newcomers. 'One person I must introduce straight away is Ann, my co-leader. She is responsible for the girls on the team and I know she'll be a great support and encourager of you all.' As Tim said this a young slim woman with long fair hair stood up and smiled around at the company. 'I'll save the other introductions until later,' Tim continued, 'because we'll be having a special get-together in the lounge this evening so that everyone can get to feel part of the team and part of the family because I want us all to feel right at the outset that we are working together as brothers and sisters doing the Lord's work and advancing his kingdom.' Tim paused for breath. 'But one important bit of business before washing up. We'll be moving the pulpit from the depot to the beach at two o'clock tomorrow, when the tide is right for building the sand up at the front – but we have to collect the depot key tonight as the manager won't be around tomorrow morning.'

He looked around. 'Er, Graham, you know the ropes. Could you pop round and pick up the keys from Mr Jenkins?'

'Yes, sure, Tim,' said a deep voice as a burly six-footer rose to his feet. 'Especially if it gets me out of the washing up,' he grinned.

Jenny turned to Liz as they began to stack the dinner plates. 'Coo! I fancy him. Really hunky!'

Liz giggled. 'You've got a one track mind, Jenny.'

'No, I haven't,' retorted Jenny in a mock-hurt tone. 'Anyway, we are on holiday. No harm in a bit of fun, is there? Seen anyone you like, then?'

Liz smiled and would not be drawn, concentrating instead on clearing the table.

As Graham returned from collecting the depot key he couldn't help hearing the raised voices from the opposite side of the road. Knowing it was none of his business he passed on, smiling. Lovers' tiff, he thought to himself. Looks like the feller's getting the worst of it.

Baz was indeed finding it hard to get a word in edge-ways. Always playing the hard man in front of his mates, he had met his match in Sandra, his girlfriend. Try as he might to calm her down and take her into the local for their usual Friday night drink, she was having none of it.

'No, I know you, Barry Holmes,' and Baz winced at the unfamiliar sound of his full name, 'you only want to get me in there so that you can palm me off and avoid giving me an answer in front of all your mates.'

'But Sand, it's not like that. You and me've got some-thing special. You know that,' Baz pleaded.

'Do I?' accused Sandra. 'I'm not sure any more. Where've you been these last three days? I've hardly seen you. You're not two-timing me, are you?'

Baz looked genuinely hurt. 'Look, girl! I've told you

over and over again. You're the only one for me and you always will be.'

'Well, where've you been then?' said Sandra, slightly soothed by Baz's reassuring tone.

'I've had business. Important things to attend to. You know how it is.' Baz tried to sound important.

'More shady business, I suppose. Why can't you get a decent job, like most men would, instead of all this thieving and things falling off backs of lorries?'

'Sshh! Keep your voice down!' hissed Baz. 'Do you want the whole town to hear you calling me a criminal? Very loyal, I must say!'

Sandra had the grace to apologise. 'I'm sorry, love,' she said, 'it's just that I sometimes wonder if we've got any future together. You've got no regular money coming in and all we ever do together is go down the pub, where I buy my own drinks. We never go out anywhere nice.'

'Look, I'm working on it. All right?' said an exasperated Baz.

But Sandra, oblivious to Baz's rising frustration, continued with the theme which had first started their quarrel. 'And now all of the girls in the office are talking about their holidays to Greece and Spain. Even Michelle's drooling over her new boyfriend and how he's taking her to Corfu next month. And what do I get? A walk along Shelham prom, that's all I get!' she whined angrily.

'I know, pet, I know,' said Baz in his best soothing tone of voice. 'Look, come and have a drink and we'll sort something out,' he coaxed her. He drew her slowly towards the pub doors, but she broke free.

'No, I will not,' she said defiantly. 'I want to know first whether you've heard a word I said – whether you're going to do anything about it. Cos if you're not,' – and she hesitated, as if summoning up her courage – 'that's the end of you and me, Baz.'

32

'What! No, you wouldn't do that, Sand!' pleaded Baz pathetically, all his bravado and guile evaporating. 'I can't lose you. You can't do this to me! I love you!' he declared, frightened by the risk of losing her into making such a rash statement.

'So you say!' Sandra's words were cold. 'But you're gonna have to prove it! If you do love me,' and her voice softened a little, 'then do something about organising a holiday for us. I've got to take my fortnight soon and I don't intend to mope around here. Either take me away somewhere nice or I'll go on my own – or maybe,' she added, 'with someone else!'

'All right, Sand, I will. I promise!' Baz whined. 'Now are you coming for that drink?'

'As long as that's clear, I will,' said Sandra, and with a sigh Baz led her into The Crown, hoping to salvage something of the evening before he planned to leave to meet Nick.

Damian returned home late that evening in an irritable mood. A car service had taken longer than anticipated at Hazeley's and Jim Evans, the foreman, had insisted that it was finished before Damian went home. Normally Damian would be able to persuade the older man that it would be better left until the morning but his charm had failed this time, which made Damian even more disgruntled. Privately he suspected that old Evans was scared of putting off another irate customer, but like it or not it was six-thirty before he could finally down tools and make his weary way home. Even so he found that he was ahead of Nick his older brother, who was normally home much earlier from his warehouse job.

'Where've you been? Mum's been throwing a wobbly over you being late. You're a naughty boy, letting your dinner spoil!' teased Damian wagging a provocative finger in Nick's face.

'Oh shut it, can't you!' snarled Nick. 'I've had things to do.'

'What things?' Damian persisted.

'Important things, and mind your own business!' warned Nick, clearly in no mood to be trifled with. He was not about to tell Damian about his last-minute discussions with Baz on their 'business venture', which had kept him busy since leaving work.

'It must be important to keep you from your food,' said Damian, as their mother entered the kitchen to catch the tail end of the conversation.

'Yes, Nick,' she agreed. 'You might have told me you were going to be so late. Your dinner's spoiling and we were begininng to worry about you.'

'Oh do stop nagging, Mum! I don't have to tell you what I'm doing all the time. You're always going on at me!' Mrs Everet's usually placid elder son was clearly on edge this evening and even Damian noticed it.

Mrs Everet was taken aback and unprepared for an argument. 'Well you might have told me this morning you were going to be late, but now you're both here we'd better eat before the dinner's burned to a crisp. Call your father, Damian.'

Comfortable again in the role she liked best, Mrs Everet busied herself in serving her home cooking to the three men in her life and after several minutes without conversation, the atmosphere mellowed again. Damian recounted his day, ready to air his opinions and grievances to anyone who would listen, and as usual found an audience with his tolerant parents, who regarded their younger son as a likeable rogue to be encouraged rather than suppressed. Nick was still tense and withdrawn and it was only at the end of the meal that he spoke again.

'Dad, do you think I could borrow the Cavalier to-night?' he asked, trying to sound as nonchalant as possible.

'What on earth for? What's the matter with your car?'

asked his surprised father.

'Well, I've been having trouble with it this week. It's broken down twice and I want to have something reliable tonight,' said a suddenly communicative Nick.

'It's a pity you didn't spend some time putting it right then,' argued Mr Everet.

'You're usually so good at looking after it,' put in his mother. 'I can't think why you had to go gallivanting off after work like you did,' she added, returning to their previous argument.

'Oh, don't start that again!' Nick almost snarled at her and the atmosphere visibly tensed once more. 'I only make a simple request and you treat it as if I'm trying to steal the crown jewels.'

'But what do you want it for?' said his father. 'What's so important that you can't stay in this evening?'

'Not you as well!' Nick snapped again. 'It's like the Spanish Inquisition! Look, can I have the car or not? I wouldn't ask if it wasn't important!'

'Well, all right, I suppose so, but mind you take care of it.' Mr Everet was essentially a mild-mannered man who hated arguments and gave way to his son rather than face another angry scene.

'Right then! I'm going to change. I'll pick up the keys on my way out,' said Nick and left the kitchen before he could be asked any more questions.

Damian too was puzzled by such uncharacteristic behaviour from his brother. Nick was usually much more placid and even-tempered than this; it must be something pretty important to make him so much on edge. 'Don't worry, Mum,' he tried to reassure her as they stacked the dishes for washing up. 'I expect he's got his first date with a new bird tonight – that's why he's jumpy.'

'Yes, I expect you're right, dear,' smiled an anxious Mrs Everet and kept her fears to herself.

~ 4 ~

Saturday, 28th July – morning

The night life of a small seaside town is a bit of an enigma and Shelham was no exception. By day, basking in its reputation of quiet middle-class respectability it gave the impression of contented sleepiness. But by night it seemed to surprise itself by becoming, for a brief period, a brightly-lit circus of social activity. It was as if it allowed the seamier side of its character to emerge each evening and even smiled benevolently on the night-time revellers, simply in order to re-establish even more strongly the next morning its all-enveloping cloak of order and decency. So by midnight the nocturnal noise and bustle had subsided and, as if by an unspoken curfew, everyone vanished indoors to leave the streets deserted and silent.

Lincoln Street was perhaps deader than most Shelham streets, and even more so by night. It was a small backwater away from the hub of things, with about a dozen privately owned terraced houses down one side facing the dull brick wall and gates of the council depot the other side. One end of the street pointed towards the centre of town while the other led through two other back streets and eventually petered out at the edge of the golf links and cliffs high above the shore. The inhabitants had been in bed some time and no lights showed from any house; only one street lamp relieved the otherwise total monotony of darkness.

At twelve thirty am a dark green Cavalier glided to a halt halfway along Lincoln Street. The lights and engine died immediately. For several minutes there was no further noise or movement, as if the car itself had gone to sleep for the night. Then both front doors opened and two figures emerged – one tall and gangly-looking, the other more squat and solid. Together they moved to the rear and opened the boot. The tall one removed a long coil of rope which he slung over his shoulder while the other lifted out what appeared to be a heavy bundle. Lowering, but not shutting, the boot lid they walked swiftly to the entrance of the council depot, two fifteen-foot high wrought-iron gates. After furtive glances in all directions, they began a whispered conversation.

'They're higher than I thought, Baz. This ain't gonna be easy.'

'Stop moaning and get on with it. This is what I brought you in on this job for. You'd better not chicken out now.'

'All right, all right. Just let me work out the best way up.' Nick studied the interwoven straight bars and decorative patterns of the gate, searching for the best foot and hand holds.

'Come on. Hurry up!' urged Baz threateningly. 'And don't forget to wait for the signal before you throw the rope over. We don't want an audience!' he hissed.

Nick said no more but gripped hard on the black painted metal of the depot gate and heaved himself up hard to gain his first foothold, the horizontal support bar five feet off the ground. That part was easy but as Nick gazed skywards he realised why for many years this padlocked entrance had been sufficient deterrent against any casual intruder. But Baz had chosen well. Nick's height, wiry strength and athletic ability were just the right combination to scale them – that and his stubborn streak which refused to be beaten.

From here on up, thought Nick, there is no easy way. Taking a deep breath he launched himself upwards, gripping and sliding with hands, knees and feet, heedless of the bruises he was collecting in the process. Somehow he finally managed to grip the top horizontal bar, heave the rest of himself up and over and slide easily down the other side of the bars. He ran to the part of the wall which he guessed was adjacent to his father's parked car, searching for a place to secure the rope. He rejected one of the council handcarts as being not solid enough and finally chose a peculiar wooden structure, built like a platform with steps on one side. Nick tested its weight and solidity and decided it would do. He attached the rope to one of the platform's thick legs, tested the knot, then turned to the wall and listened. All was quiet, but within seconds came the sound Nick expected, a low owl-like whistle, the all-clear signal from Baz.

He peered up now at the wall, studying for the first time the solid black outline against the blue-black night sky beyond. From this close it looked massive and unassailable and Nick wondered whether Baz had miscalculated and would be unable to climb it, even with a rope. Then he remembered those arm-wrestling contests in the pub when Baz would take on all comers and win, and he realised that Baz would be reckoning on his strength of arm to compensate for his foot. The signal came again from Baz, more urgent and impatient this time.

'All right, all right,' muttered Nick and steadied himself to throw the rope. He glanced again at the wall and took a deep breath. He coiled the rope carefully, checking for any snags to its running out freely, then stepped back. He ran forward two paces and jumped in the air as his right hand shot forward like a javelin thrower's and the rope whirled up into the darkness and disappeared the other side of the wall.

Nick smiled smugly to himself at his success. He hoped Baz would get his part right; sure enough a minute later he felt two tugs on the rope and immediately began hauling it back up the wall. Baz's bundle was certainly heavy but moved smoothly until it stuck near the top. Nick had to release and pull again several times before the bundle freed itself and came sailing over the wall. Too late, Nick saw with horror the heavy weight plummet down well away from his reach and clatter on the concrete with a noise like a train door slamming. He froze, not daring to retrieve it, and was only dimly aware that a car door had clicked outside and that Baz had bolted for cover.

It was some minutes before anything else moved and Nick seriously wondered if Baz had deserted him. But then came the low whistle and Nick breathed again. He hurriedly retrieved the bundle, untied the rope, and re-coiled it ready for his second throw. He repeated his first throw and the rope sailed up. But in his haste he had not been as careful and the rope caught on itself, hit the top of the wall and slithered back in an ungainly heap.

Nick cursed himself for being such a fool. Panic was the worst thing in this situation – you only made mistakes. Carefully now he recoiled the rope, checking and re-checking his preparations and ignoring the impatient whistle from Baz. He coiled himself and sprang again; this time there was no mistake and the rope snaked down the outside of the wall. He breathed a sigh of relief and allowed himself the luxury of relaxing for a few minutes. The next part was up to Baz.

He leant against the platform and waited for his partner

to scale the wall. He checked the ground below it where Baz would land for any dangerous object – he didn't want an accomplice with a broken ankle. Come to think of it, it was still a very long drop for Baz, with his dodgy foot. Nick looked around. Of course, the hand carts. He wheeled one beneath the rope. Gauging the height of the wall he did some rough calculations. The cart was three feet high, Baz was about six feet; that still left him a drop of about six feet. Still it would have to do.

Baz's head appeared and his leg swung over the top of the wall. Nick hissed up at him. 'I've got a hand cart here for you to land on – it's a long drop. It's on wheels so I'll hold it steady but make sure you land in the middle.'

Baz said nothing but seemed to nod in agreement and made to descend the wall. His arms easily held his weight as his legs dropped lower and lower. A pause while he hung motionless and Nick moved the cart a fraction to be exactly beneath him. Then noiselessly Baz's feet descended again, gaining momentum. Nick braced himself as Baz hit the cart with both feet. He staggered, overbalanced and fell backwards. Nick darted forward, grabbed Baz's flailing arm and together they collapsed to the ground.

'Are you OK?'

There was no immediate answer from Baz as the heavier man sat up and gingerly felt his various joints.

'Yeah, no thanks to you, and keep your voice down,' he finally grunted back to Nick.

Some gratitude! thought Nick as he lifted Baz up. 'Your tools are over here,' he whispered.

'Haven't you undone them yet?' grunted Baz as he saw Nick struggling with the knots. 'Fat lot of good you are. Come on. Give them here!'

Nick's temper rose but he decided against arguing; this was definitely not the time or place. He watched uncomfortably as Baz unknotted the bag, selected a large crowbar and a torch and led the way to the office situated at the far side of the yard well away from the area of the gates, ideal for their purposes. The torchlight made the depot yard far less eerie and Nick felt his confidence return. Suddenly Baz hissed, 'You idiot! You've left the rope there for every Tom, Dick or Harry to see!'

Nick saw their mistake. The rope was still hanging over the wall, a dead giveaway if anyone came along. He quickly retrieved it, realising with a grim smile that Baz was never likely to admit it might be his oversight too. Baz meanwhile was surveying the door to the tiny two-roomed office building which served as work-place for Mr Jenkins the manager, when he was there, and Yvonne, whose witless chatter had given Baz the idea for the robbery. The door looked solid enough in heavy oak but Baz smiled.

'Yale. We'll only need one crow, and it shouldn't make too much noise.'

He substituted his original choice for a smaller crowbar in his bag and levered it down between the door and the jamb. There was a splintering of wood; Baz gave a sudden heave and the door flew open as the lock hung uselessly on its now protruding screws.

'Well done, Baz, that was easy enough.'

'That was nothing. The real job's inside.' He led the way through the outer room into the manager's office. The searching torchlight soon discovered the grey bulk of the safe squatting in the far corner.

'That's going to be the difficult bit,' Baz grimaced as he examined the blank exterior of the box that held their fortune. He dumped his bag, laying the torch on top.

'Shut both the doors and come and give us a hand,' he ordered.

When Nick returned he found Baz struggling to move

the safe. He joined him and together they inched it out from the wall.

'That'll do,' said Baz. 'Lucky for us it wasn't fixed to the floor. Some of them are. Now let's push it over, face down. Ready?'

Together they heaved it over, the crash splintering a floorboard and the noise like thunder scaring Nick in case they were heard until he remembered Baz's precaution in getting him to shut the doors.

'Now what? You still haven't got into the safe,' Nick pointed out unnecessarily.

'No, you berk, but the back of the safe is always made from thinner metal, isn't it? Now shut up and hand me that drill.'

For the next half hour Baz worked at the back of the safe under the torchlight held by Nick, using a variety of cold chisels, hammers and drills from the bag of tools he had brought. Nick had permanent jitters, expecting any moment someone to come seeking the cause of the loud banging to which Baz seemed oblivious. Only once did he voice a complaint about Baz being rather amateurish but wished he hadn't when he heard Baz's withering reply.

'What did you expect, pea-brain? A lump of gelignite and a loud bang, like in the pictures? So that the neighbours wake up, call the police and we're caught red-handed! And where do we get gelly without passing the word through the criminal world that we're on a job? Then the snouts get to hear of it, they tell the pigs – sorry police – and we walk into their trap. No, thickhead, this isn't the TV, with guns and fast cars where the cops always get their man. This is the real world where crime happens all the time and small-time crooks like you and me don't get nicked because we stay small and aren't afraid of a bit of grafting to get what we want. Now hold that torch still, I'm nearly through this bit.'

And apart from that burst Baz said little else until, with a final twist of his crowbar, he levered off enough of the backplate to give access to the safe's contents. Feverishly he ransacked the safe, strewing the floor with papers and files until finally he sat back on his haunches.

'There you are! What did I tell you?' Baz flourished a fat wad of five pound notes in Nick's face, his perspiring face aglow with triumph.

'Wow! Brilliant, Baz! Is there any more?'

'Yeah, some coin bags. Get 'em out quick and then let's go. We've been here long enough.'

Nick pulled out three large bags of coins and two further bundles of notes. 'Blimey! These are really heavy, Baz!'

'Well, what did you expect? People pay for their deck chairs with small change. The council aren't going to change it all into ten pound notes just for our convenience, are they? Now cut out the gassing. Put these notes into one of the bags and let's get going. We've been lucky so far but we don't wanna take any unnecessary chances.'

'Lucky? I thought you said you'd got this all planned.'

'I did! But nothing's certain. We've left that car out there a long time and there's always a risk involved if someone comes along. Shine that torch over here – I can't see to do up my tools!'

Nick nervously obeyed and was glad that the job was nearly over. Baz's words had hardly reassured him and he'd be glad to get out of the place. Baz seemed to have nerves of steel, but then he was used to this sort of thing. Nick led the way out of the office, torch in one hand, money bags in the other. It was awkward opening the first door with his hands full but the broken outer door was easier – he kicked that aside with ease but in his haste knocked it hard against the wall.

'Idiot!' hissed Baz. 'Do you want to wake the whole street?'

'Sorry,' Nick mouthed in reply and continued out of the doorway and over to the wall. He searched around for the rope with the torch. As he bent down to pick it up, Baz's hand gripped his shoulder and whispered in his ear, 'Freeze!'

Fortunately Nick had his wits about him and instantly switched off the torch and very slowly unbent. By now he could hear it too, the slow measured tread of a pedestrian walking the length of Lincoln Street just the other side of the wall. Nick looked at Baz and the other's expression confirmed his own fears. That steady unhurried walk was not that of someone hurrying home from a late night; it was the pace of someone at work, on duty – police! They listened spellbound as the sound approached the gates. Had the man heard Nick bang that door? Had he seen a glimmer from his torch? Nick hoped fervently that the man had been too far away to have done either.

At the gates the boots halted. The next sound was the gates being rattled as the constable tested the padlock and chain. How glad they both were at Baz's insistence of not cutting the chain! Then the yard behind them was suddenly spotted with light. They ducked quickly behind a cart as the police torch winked its way around the yard. Was this routine or was the man suspicious of something? They watched, horrified, as the torch swept nearer the open office door, a certain giveaway if the copper spotted it. Then the light disappeared and a moment later they could hear the sound of footsteps receding into the distance.

Baz let out a long sigh of relief. 'I thought we'd had it that time,' he whispered. 'We'll give him a couple more minutes but I think we've got away with this one.'

Nick was still petrified and couldn't speak. He could

44

only marvel at Baz's coolness and when he did eventually speak he was still trembling. 'I was sure he'd heard us. How do you know he didn't see the door?' Baz gently laughed at Nick's terrified expression. Nick, annoyed, burst out, angrily, 'How can you be so calm? We nearly got caught. We'd have ended up in jail for this!'

'So what?' laughed Baz. 'That's the risk you take. Sometimes you win – sometimes you lose,' he ended meaningfully.

'You mean – you've been inside!' gasped Nick.

'Sure – no need to look so shocked. What did you expect? Or does it offend you to be associated with a jailbird?'

Nick was stunned at how Baz took even arrest and prison so lightly. For the second time he wondered why he was doing this, and he couldn't resist a sarcastic throw-away line at Baz.

'No wonder you can't get a job if you've got a record.'

'Shut up, big mouth, or I'll shut it for you! Just remember who's getting you a half share of five thousand quid. I'll bet you won't be too stuck up to accept two and a half grand, even if it is from a jailbird.' He paused, listening. 'Anyway, sucker, it's time we were going. That copper's had his two minutes and it sounds like it's all clear.'

'How do we get out of here?'

'Berk! Don't you remember anything? It's like I planned it. Climb those gates again with the rope and attach it to the car door frame. Throw the rope over and I'll attach the tools and the money. Then I come over last. Don't mess it up!'

'OK, I'm off,' said Nick, relieved to be in action again.

'Wait a minute. Where did you put the money?'

'Oh yeah. It's over here,' and Nick hurriedly gathered up the bags from where he had dropped them when the policeman had arrived, and handed over the precious booty.

'Right. Now get going!' ordered Baz.

Damian had spent a frustrating evening. He had gone out of his way to spoil Shirley on the last night of her holiday, or so he thought, but she wasn't acting grateful in the way that he had hoped. They had made the grand tour of all the amusement arcades (he'd even won for her one of those cute little blue teddy bears on the rifle range, though it had cost him almost as much in paying for the attempts at it as the bear was probably worth!) He had bought her expensive drinks in one of the more exclusive pubs in town and they had topped that off with late-night fish and chips which they had eaten together, strolling along the beach in the warm darkness. Shirley had wanted to stay longer – she had said something slushy like wanting to listen to the gentle rhythm of the tide, which Damian didn't understand but dismissed as girl-talk. He had insisted that they continue their walk up the cliff beside the golf links – because of the view, he told her, though his real reason was to get Shirley alone. It had led to the first cooling of their intimacy that evening; though he thought he had handled it manfully she considered that ignoring her wishes was unfeeling and chauvinistic. So she had gone unwillingly and the colourful panoramic view of the town's lights, the white surf and the distant lighthouse had only just restored her good humour and tenderness towards her holiday romance.

Damian had chosen his spot well (it was not the first time he had planned this sort of evening). He had guided Shirley to a small hollow high up and away from the path where they were sheltered from the wind but could still see down to the sea and shoreline of Shelham. They had been happy for a while making small talk and enjoying the view. Shirley relaxed and began to feel quite affectionate towards the boy who had after all made her holiday a lot more fun and deserved some return for all the money and time he had invested in giving her a good time. So when he turned to kiss her she found it natural to return it. It had seemed natural too when his hands began to caress and fondle, first her hair, then her arms, then other parts of her body. She felt herself drifting and floating, enjoying the sweet sensation of timelessness. Then the sound of other walkers on the path above had disturbed them. Shirley had tensed, sat up and shivered. She broke away from Damian to reach for her jacket.

The romantic atmosphere had evaporated with the interruption and Shirley announced in a frosty voice that it was time she went home. It had taken all of Damian's persuasive powers to make her stay longer and no matter how much he coaxed or promised he could never regain the intimacy with her he was enjoying when they were interrupted. In the end he had lost his patience and called her various names for not letting him have his way and accused her of ingratitude for not repaying him all the money he'd spent. This had sent Shirley into floods of tears and he had then to cope with what threatened to be a very embarrassing scene. She recognised the injustice of his remarks but was upset at the shattering of her illusions. She had felt cheap and used – he had called her a tart because he expected her to act like one, to be bought for the price of a few drinks. It had taken Damian a long time to calm her down and it was almost a relief when she accepted his offer to walk her home.

Fortunately it was not far and Damian knew a more direct route through some back streets at the foot of the cliffs. They walked in silence, neither wanting to talk for fear of the other's reactions. Shirley, in her hurting, even refused to walk beside him, but stayed a pace or two behind. Damian led the way down Links Close leading into Brownhill Road. But as he turned the corner into Lincoln Street he froze at the sight which met his eyes and Shirley almost collided with him.

'What's the mat . . .?' she began to ask as Damian quickly wheeled and clasped a hand over her mouth, dragging her back round the corner as he did so and pinning her against the side wall of the end house. She struggled, suspicious again of his motives until he regained his presence of mind and whispered in her ear.

'There's a courting couple round the corner – we don't want them to see us. We'll wait here – they'll be gone in a minute.'

He took his hand from her mouth and Shirley relaxed. Damian edged back towards the corner and gingerly peered down Lincoln Street again to confirm what he thought he had seen, two men engaged in what appeared to be a highly illegal activity. Yes, they were still there. By the light of the solitary street lamp Damian could see them clearly, one sitting on top of the wall of the council depot and the other standing on the pavement by a dark-coloured Cavalier. As he watched, the man on the wall drew up the rope behind him which evidently had a heavy weight on the end. The rope ended in a large bundle which he then threw to the man below, before lowering himself and dropping to the pavement.

He seemed to fall badly and the other man came to his aid. As he turned to help his partner Damian caught sight of his face in the lamplight and gasped in horror – his brother Nick!

Shirley heard his indrawn breath and came up beside him. 'What is it? Can I look?' she whispered.

'No, you can't!' he hissed. 'Stay back there out of sight and I'll tell you when they've gone.' Stunned by his ferocity she meekly obeyed.

Damian looked again down the street but had only time to see the men climb into the car and drive off. But there was no mistaking what he had seen and it shocked him rigid. His brother, a thief? Damian had little enough time for the law, but this was heavy stuff!

'I take it they've gone then, whoever they were,' said Shirley emerging to stand beside him. 'What was going on?'

'Oh, nothing much,' he replied off-handedly and despite her badgering him for more information Damian remained uncommunicative the rest of the way back, brooding on his very troubled thoughts.

~ 5 ~

Saturday, 28th July – afternoon

'Thank goodness that's finished!' said Al, as he threw down the last spanner into his tool box and wiped his hands on an oily rag. 'That one was a brute. Still, what can you expect with foreign cars?' he proclaimed to anyone who would listen in Hazeley's Garage.

'You're lucky you didn't have the one I serviced last night,' rejoined Damian. 'Old Evans kept me here until 6.30,' he grumbled, 'and then he had the nerve to tick me off for being five minutes late this morning.'

'It was a quarter of an hour, actually,' Al corrected him, 'but never mind,' he quickly added as Damian shot him a warning look. 'I just hope it, or rather she, was all worth it.'

'What do you mean?' growled Damian. He was in a disagreeable mood because of his lack of sleep and experiences of the night before, as Al had rightly guessed.

'Oh come off it, Daim! You know, what's-er-name, your bit of stuff, the one from Birmingham, last night of her holiday and all that. You were full of it yesterday, though you're very quiet about it today. How'd it go?'

'Oh, all right,' said Damian, unusually reticent.

50

'All right!?' echoed Al. 'Is that all you're going to say? I expected a blow by blow account to keep us amused all morning. Went wrong, did it? She wouldn't let you, I bet – or did she stand you up?' Al chortled.

Normally Damian would have been equal to such bantering and quite capable of inventing a description of the whole evening for their entertainment. But what he had seen in Lincoln Street last night had sobered even him and he was content to let Al think what he liked.

'Yeah! It was all right,' he repeated. His blue eyes flashed piercingly at Al as if daring him to question further.

'OK,' said Al, knowing Damian's unpredictable moods. He changed the subject. 'Coming down for a pint, then? It's near enough knocking off time.'

'Yeah. Why not? I've had enough of this place for one week.'

Al hoped his suggestion would improve Damian's temper and if he bought the drinks he might even persuade Damian to reveal what really happened between him and Shirley. The lunchtime pie and pint certainly revived Damian's spirits but try as he might, Al could get no information from him.

'Oh well,' he said at last. 'I must be off if I'm going to do my shopping.'

'What? Oh yes, your new suit.' Damian's memory was still sharp, as was his sense of fun. 'Hang on, I'm coming too. I don't want to miss this. You in a suit!' And he hooted at Al as they left The Fox. Al smiled ruefully but even a friend like Damian was better than no friend at all when he was buying clothes and Al was secretly relieved that Damian decided to tag along.

But Al was out of luck. Unwin's sale had been popular that morning and by the time Al arrived he could find no suit at all to fit him without paying the earth for it. He left the shop somewhat deflated and they wandered through the lunch time crowds at rather a loose end. It was Damian who spotted the strange little procession weaving its way towards them through the crowds and traffic, pushing a very rusty trailer which had obviously seen better days.

'Hey! What do you make of that ?'

'What?' said Al blankly and when he followed Damian's pointing finger he could only add, 'I dunno. Some nuts pushing a trailer.'

'Oh, come on!' coaxed Damian. 'Let's go and find out what gives. Might be a bit of fun!' And he stepped off the kerb. Al was rather bemused by Damian's idea of fun but anything would be better than a Saturday afternoon with nothing to do, he figured.

Graham halted the trailer just in time to avoid colliding with the tall blond youth who had just stepped out in front of them.

'Hi! What are you doing?' began Damian, never at a loss for words.

'We're on our way to collect something on this trailer,' replied Graham easily, amused at this stranger's curiosity but equally undaunted. He was used to people asking the Mission team what they were up to, and no wonder, considering some of the crazy things they did!

'Must be pretty big if you need that great chariot to carry it,' Damian persisted.

'It is. We're collecting a pulpit to take it down to the beach.'

'A pulpit! You only find those in churches, don't you?'

Graham laughed. 'This is a beach pulpit. We're taking it to the beach for our beach meetings which start tomorrow. Why don't you come along and help if you're interested?' That'll get rid of him for sure, he thought.

To his surprise Damian replied, 'Yeah. OK. Why not? We don't mind lending a hand, do we Al?' Al didn't look at all sure, thought Graham, but he was anxious to be off and so responded breezily.

'Well, there's a space behind me if you want to help push. But we're in a bit of a hurry so we must get on.' And steering round Damian, Graham set the trailer in motion again.

'Come on, Al!' grinned Damian, and dragging Al by the arm he found space for them both at the side of the trailer, laughing off all Al's muttered comments about the craziness of what they were doing. Graham smiled to himself at the whispered conversation taking place behind him. Not for the first time someone had got roped into helping the mission without really knowing what they were letting themselves in for. Graham fully expected the two youths to vanish once they realised this involved some hard work.

They eventually managed to leave the crowded High Street behind and their passage was much smoother the nearer they got to their destination. Graham steered the trailer expertly around corners and parked cars and the corner of Lincoln Street soon came into view. Unknown to him their route was having an increasingly unsettling effect on Damian. The nearer they approached the council depot the more nervous Damian was becoming and was regretting his earlier enthusiasm for helping out. To re-visit so soon the scene of the crime he had so dramatically witnessed was unnerving and he dreaded the thought of what they might find there. Visions of smashed-up doors and general chaos formed themselves in Damian's mind. Maybe the police already knew and would be swarming all over the place like bees round a honey pot. The possibilities were various and all of them terrible; vainly he searched for a way out of the trap he had made for himself. Even Al noticed the change in Damian's behaviour, and was intrigued how his moods could alter so quickly.

'Cheer up, Daim. You look like you've seen a ghost,'

he quipped, but Damian wouldn't rise to the bait. 'Not scared of a bit of hard work, are you? You were the one who volunteered us, remember?'

'No, it's not that, it's . . .' but as Damian searched for the words he had another shock. They had halted by the depot gates and Graham had gone to unlock the chain with the key he had collected last night. And there was nothing wrong! Any moment Damian expected him to cry out or raise the alarm, but Graham was acting perfectly normally as he swung the gates wide.

'Come on then. Bring her in!' he called and the rusty old trailer rolled unwillingly up the slope pushed by seven young pairs of hands. 'Right. Now take it over there, will you?' he said, pointing to the far corner of the yard. 'They've moved the pulpit but I can just spot it over by the wall. Leslie and Jim, would you clear a path through – you'll have to push the handcarts right out of the way. Good. Now let's get this trailer as near as we can. Fine. OK. There she is – good old Bertha!' and he jokingly patted the large wooden structure. Little did he realise that a few hours earlier 'Bertha' had been used for a very different purpose.

'Right, we need all the hands we can get,' Graham continued. He turned to the two mechanics. 'Sorry, I didn't ask your names.'

'I'm Al and he's Damian,' said Al, taking charge as Damian seemed rather overawed by things at the moment.

'Well, if you two can manage that corner it should be a piece of cake. Ready now everyone – lift!' And Bertha did lift, the first time she'd been moved for nearly a year. Even with so many hands it was a struggle to position the heavy pulpit centrally on the trailer.

'Phew!' remarked Andy. 'That was hard work!'

'We haven't really started yet,' laughed Graham. 'Now hold it steady, or she'll fall off again. Paul, if you grab some of those ropes over there we can tie it down. That should stop it slipping off. Oh, I nearly forgot. We'll need some sandbags for building up the front.' He looked round and chose the nearest person for the task. 'Damian, could you grab about a dozen of those hessian bags lying over there by the wall?'

'Yeah, sure.' Damian had found his voice again. Working as a team was quite fun and made hard work much easier. He walked quickly to the spot Graham had indicated and rummaged around for the required twelve bags. Suddenly he froze, and his fears returned. There on the ground in full view, lay three huge bundles of banknotes. He knew at once what they were, though how they got there he had no idea. He stared at them aghast, too petrified to move. How could Nick have been such a fool?! Stealing money was bad enough, but losing it again was even worse! What was he supposed to do now? The notes seemed to stare back at him from the ground, accusing him, daring him to do something to cover up the evidence.

'Found them, Damian?' called out Graham's voice. 'Give him a hand, would you, Jim?' he added.

Damian panicked. Hopes of covering the money up again vanished as he heard Jim's footsteps approaching. What could he do? The huge wad was too big for his pocket and anyway would leave a large tell-tale bulge. What then? Think quickly! Jim was right behind him.

In desperation he swooped one of the bags over the money and, as he pretended to gather up more bags, he pushed the bundles down into the dark safe depths of the sandbag. He straightened up as Jim arrived.

'Need any help?' smiled Jim.

'Er– I've got about eight here,' said Damian, trying not to sound too flustered. 'I think there are some more over there.'

Jim quickly helped complete the task and together they

returned to the others, who had just finished roping down the pulpit. With a few false starts and much laughter they manoeuvred the now laden trailer back out of the yard and began the bumpy journey to the beach. Damian walked as in a dream, fighting hard to quell the feeling of nausea in the pit of his stomach and to regain his composure. He took stock of what had happened. He had saved the robbery from being discovered and given his brother more time to cover his tracks – though why I should bother to help Nick, I don't know, he reflected. So far, so good. But what if someone found the money in the sandbag? That would be even worse and might even point the finger at him. He had better stick around and do what he could to protect his own interests and to keep his guilty secret hidden at all costs.

Ten minutes later they were wheeling the trailer down the ramp which led from the promenade to the pebbles of the beach. The wheels promptly sank and came to an abrupt halt. From there the pulpit would have to be carried twenty yards across the shingle to its resting place for the next fortnight. Al was just wondering how they were going to manage that when it seemed they were descended upon by twenty more people of all shapes and sizes, all eager to help carry the pulpit, like some trophy of war, to its holiday home. The rest of the Mission team had been waiting for them on the beach and the chatter and laughter rose in a great swell as the huge structure was borne along.

'Hello, I'm Jenny. I've not met you before, have I?' said Jenny to Al as they lifted and stumbled their way.

Al was taken aback by the openness of the girl before him. 'No, I'm not with your lot. Me and Damian – that's my mate over there – just came along for a bit of a laugh, really.'

'Oh good,' smiled Jenny. 'And is it?'

'Is it what?' said Al, feeling rather awkward.

'Is it a laugh?'

'Oh. Well yes, I suppose it is, really. You all certainly seem to be enjoying yourselves.'

'Oh yes. It's hard work. We've been on the go since eight o'clock this morning, but it's great fun, and everyone's made me feel very welcome. It's my first time with the beach mission, you see,' Jenny volunteered.

'Oh, I see.' Al said no more but when he could he stole sidelong glances at the vivacious girl who had caught his attention. It was not just her blonde hair and figure that Al found attractive, but her lively interest and openness. Jenny had already noticed that she had made a hit and gave him friendly smiles whenever she could break away from sand carrying. Al was bowled over. None of the girls he knew behaved in such a friendly way towards him. He was now very willing to help in the task of setting up the pulpit.

Damian meanwhile was having great difficulty in keeping track of all the sandbags. There were so many pairs of hands eager to join in the fun of ferrying buckets down to the sand, conveyor-belting them full of sand back to the pulpit and filling the empty sandbags, that he had no chance of finding *the* sandbag again, still less of keeping it safe from prying eyes. All he could do was to stand watching helplessly, occasionally helping to hold open a sandbag to be filled, expecting and dreading any moment to hear a cry of discovery from somewhere around him. Miraculously, that cry never came. Somehow, without his realising the moment, the last sandbag had been filled and the discovery had not been made. There they all stood like khaki soldiers leaning drunkenly in a row, all apparently the same, but with one infinitely more valuable than all the rest. Which one? Damian couldn't begin to guess but inwardly breathed a sigh of relief that his secret was safe.

For the Mission team the fun was not over. While

some continued to ferry sand up the beach, a small team got busy arranging the weighty bags around the foot and sides of the pulpit's front. The whole of the front side of the structure consisted of a sloping wooden board, cleverly designed with horizontal ridges to be faced with sand. When enough sand had been placed on the board and held up by the sandbags the whole front of the pulpit resembled an enormous sandcastle. This could then be decorated in various ways to transform even a cloudy high-tide day into a scene of summer sun and sand. The team responsible for this soon had the sand covering the boards and began to add ferns and seaside flowers. The final touch was given by two girls using attractive pebbles to spell out on the sand the words 'I am the way.'

Now that the flurry of work was dying down and members of the team were drifting off in twos and threes to paddle or sunbathe, Al tried to attract Jenny's attention again. She was chatting animatedly to another girl of about the same height and age, obviously a close friend. Seeing the two girls together gave Al an idea and he looked around for Damian, who was now idly watching the pulpit being decorated.

'Hey, Daim,' he beckoned.

Damian looked up casually. How much more relaxed he felt now compared to half an hour ago. 'Hi, Al! Looks good, doesn't it?' he grinned, nodding towards the pulpit.

'Never mind that,' said Al impatiently. 'I've seen this gorgeous bird – well two actually – and you and me could make a hit there if we play it right.'

'Oh, yes, and what's mine like? – face like the back of a bus, I suppose.'

'She's got dark hair, gorgeous brown eyes, lovely slim figure.' Al made it up as he went along and noticed the flicker of light in Damian's face, interested despite himself and his sour experience with Shirley.

58

'Aw, I don't know that I can be bothered, and anyway I might cramp your style!' teased Damian.

'Oh, come on! Quit stalling. They'll go in a minute.' And Damian allowed himself to be half pulled along the beach, amused at Al's sudden keenness, unusual for someone usually so laid back.

When they reached the girls, Damian was grateful for Al's persistence. The Liz he was introduced to turned out to be extremely good looking. It seemed too by the way she returned his smile that she was interested in him as well. He slipped into easy conversation with her, appearing interested in everything she said but missing no opportunity to impress her with casual references to himself and his lifestyle. Liz listened politely and seemed in no hurry to get rid of him. There was a certain reserve about her but to Damian, smarting from his experiences with Shirley, that only increased her attractiveness.

Al, too, was progressing well in his friendship with Jenny. He found it easy to impress her because she wanted to be impressed and seemed eager to encourage his overtures. He was determined to arrange a date with her and tried to move Jenny away from Damian and Liz.

'So what job do you do?' Damian was asking Liz.

'Oh, I've just left the sixth form. I'm hoping to go to Art College next term if my grades are high enough.'

'Oh,' Damian replied, realising he was a little out of his depth. 'So what do you do on this mission of yours?'

'Well, we run activities for all ages. Jenny and I are going to be helping with the K Club – that's for older teenagers. It's going to be fun – we meet in an old garage and play music and stuff. We spent this morning doing it up – it looks really great – you should come along.'

'We might just do that.' Al's ears had pricked up at what he thought was Liz's personal invitation and was eager to get in on the action himself. 'Where is this K Club then?'

'Just behind the house in Augustine Street. You can't miss it. It starts at eight o'clock.'

'Yes, you must come too, Al,' invited Jenny. 'I'll be there, and I'll even let you buy me a drink.' She gave him a knowing smile. It was clear that both Al and Jenny were equally keen on seeing each other again and this seemed a perfect opportunity.

'Good. That's agreed then,' said Liz, slightly alarmed at the looks Al and Jenny were giving each other. 'We've got to go now. Back to the house for tea,' she explained hastily, as she took Jenny's reluctant arm and marched her off the beach.

'You did all right there, mate,' admitted Damian as they watched them go. 'My one's a little cracker.'

'Yeah, they're both good lookers,' agreed Al. 'I just hope we're not getting involved in anything too religious.'

'Nothing I can't handle,' Damian boasted. 'And I can handle her any time!' And with a raucous laugh at his own coarse joke he ran off along the beach turning to taunt Al with a few well-aimed pebbles.

Graham had left the beach ten minutes earlier in order to return to the depot the ropes they had borrowed. Lincoln Street was quiet as he unlocked the chain again and the deserted yard had almost an eerie atmosphere as he walked to the spot where the ropes belonged. The silence almost gave him the creeps and an involuntary shiver trickled down his spine. Laughing at his own foolishness he gazed around to reassure himself that everything was normal. Yes, everything was as it should be and he turned back to coil the ropes neatly.

Suddenly his memory did a double take and his eyes flitted back to the office door. He was right – it was ajar. Unusual, he thought, on a Saturday afternoon. His curiosity got the better of him and he went closer. Then he noticed the splintered door jamb and his uneasiness increased. Still, having got this far, I'd better see what's what, he reasoned to himself and so did what he later regretted bitterly. He pushed the door open slowly and entered the outer office. It seemed undisturbed and Graham began to think that his suspicions were unfounded after all. But when he opened the second door his suspicions hardened to certainty, for there all around lay the evidence of the crime – the battered safe and the contents strewn over the floor. There was also a telephone hanging by its cord over the side of the desk and in his state of shock he did what in normal circumstances would have been perfectly natural. He picked the phone up and replaced it in its proper position on the desk.

It was at that moment that he thought he heard a noise. Re-entering the outer office he peered round the half-open door to discover he was not alone! A man was standing in the middle of the yard gazing around. Fortunately his back was towards the office and Graham quietly pushed the door to. He now realised the embarrassing predicament he was in and stood with bated breath, praying that the man would not approach the office.

For several minutes he heard nothing and at last plucked up courage to look out again. The yard was deserted once more and Graham almost wondered if he had daydreamed the man. But now was not the time for such questioning and he lost no time in getting out of the place. With trembling hands he re-locked the gates and quickly put as much distance as he could between himself and Lincoln Street.

He tried to calm the rising panic within him and decide on his next course. He knew he should tell the police but what if the man had seen him enter the office? That could put him in a very awkward position. The burglary would be discovered anyway, sooner or later, and he could plead ignorance of the whole affair, which was of course true. The simplest thing, he decided, would be to act as if he had seen nothing and act normally.

But the keys! Of course, he had promised to return them to Mr Jenkins before five o'clock, as the manager would be out for the evening and wanted to be sure of their safe return. Nothing for it then but to retrace his steps to the manager's house.

Five minutes later, Graham was knocking on Mr Jenkins' door. 'Keep calm,' he told himself. 'Act as if nothing has happened.'

'Oh, hello, Mr Jenkins. Your keys – all safe and sound.'

'Did you find everything you wanted then, son?' asked the kindly-looking grey-haired manager.

'Oh yes – fine. No problem. We got it down to the beach. No trouble. It was – er– well – you know – fine.'

'Oh good,' concluded Mr Jenkins. His brows furrowed as he watched Graham leave and puzzled as to why the confident young man of the night before had become so awkward and nervous over a simple matter of returning some keys. Shaking his head he returned indoors to his half-eaten tea.

~ 6 ~

Saturday, 28th July – evening

That day Fred Jenkins felt he was doomed never to finish his tea. He had been sitting down for only about ten minutes when his front door bell rang again. Wearily he rose, took a gulp from his mug of tea to wash down the last mouthful of food, muttered something about a wife who would deal with callers coming in handy at a time like this, and went to answer the door.

'Hello, Bob! This is a surprise. Is this a social call or is it you don't see enough of me Monday to Friday?'

'Evening, Mr Jenkins,' said Bob Clement with a sheepish grin. 'Sorry to trouble you but it's a bit strange like,' he ended rather lamely, unsure how to continue.

'What's strange, Bob? You'd better come in and tell me.' For the second time in a quarter of an hour, Fred Jenkins' brow creased in perplexity, but he knew his workman well enough to know something was wrong.

Bob seemed to relax a little behind the closed front door. 'It's just that I had to pass through Lincoln Street this afternoon on my way home and I couldn't believe it. The depot gates were open!'

'It's all right. I expect it was the lad from the Beach

Mission. He borrowed the keys to get their pulpit out of the yard.'

'But there was no one there, Mr Jenkins. I checked in the yard – it was deserted.'

Fred Jenkins sighed. He knew he would have to go and check it even though there was probably nothing amiss. 'All right, Bob. Hang on a minute, can you? I'll just put some shoes on and I'll be with you.' He sighed again, thinking of his uneaten tea. Still it would probably be too cold now, anyway.

Nick was five minutes late for his appointment with Baz that evening. That put an edge on Baz's temper for he had been chafing impatiently all day for this meeting.

'Come on. Where've you been? I've been waiting all day for you and now you're late as well.'

'Well it was your idea to wait till now. Cause less suspicion you said. Too risky to come up here in the daytime. People might wonder what we were up to, you said,' Nick repeated, for emphasis.

'All right, all right. But you've got the stuff with you now?'

'Yeah, of course I have. But it wasn't easy, transferring all the loot and your gear from the Cavalier into the Escort. I was scared stiff someone might see me.'

'Don't be such a chicken. I had my doubts about you last night. You nearly blew it then!'

'That's rubbish. I did my part all right. And I've taken all the risks since then.'

'Look, stop arguing and let's get the stuff inside. I'll take the money!'

Baz was in no mood to be crossed and they carried the contents of Nick's boot into the deserted farmhouse. Even so, Nick gave a furtive look up and down the disused track, though he knew that no-one ever visited these long-forgotten buildings.

They picked their way over the debris into the room which Baz had made his own. Clever the way Baz has deliberately left the place looking squalid so no-one would know that he lives here, thought Nick. He laid Baz's tools down in one corner and helped clear a space in the middle of the floor for what they were both eagerly awaiting: the counting of the money.

They took a bag each and emptied the contents. Some coins had been separately bagged but much of it was just a mountain of loose change and it was a slow laborious job to separate and count it all.

Baz soon tired of all the mental arithmetic involved. 'Give us the other bag, Nick. I'll count the notes. That's much more my style,' he chortled.

Nick passed the bag and without looking up continued to count the pile of ten pences in front of him.

'Where are they then?' interrupted him in the middle of his count.

'Where's what?' he said unthinking.

'The notes, thick head! What do you think I mean?'

'I haven't got them.' Nick stopped counting and looked up.

'Well, they're not here!' said Baz fiercely. 'You must have them in your bag.'

'No, I haven't!' They looked at each other in alarm for two frozen seconds before they scrabbled frantically around the floor for the missing money. To no avail. They sat back on their haunches in disbelief.

Baz suddenly exploded. 'The car boot!' and he dashed through the doorway a split second before Nick to retrieve the notes, desperately convincing themselves that they must be in the old Escort. It was no use. Try as they might, the money was not to be found there, or anywhere else in Nick's car. They returned to the house, Baz kicking angrily at anything that lay in his path. Nick felt he would have kicked him if he'd been in the way.

'Wait a minute!' Baz turned on Nick. 'You must have left them in the other car.'

'I wish I had,' said Nick disconsolately. 'But I searched Dad's car boot thoroughly. You don't think I'd be daft enough to leave anything there for Dad to find, do you?' It's no good, Baz,' he continued, 'somehow, I don't know how, we must have left them behind – in the street maybe.'

Baz's eyes widened in horror at the thought, then suddenly narrowed accusingly at Nick. 'No!' he said slowly. 'I know where they are – they're still back in that blinking yard. Don't you remember when that flatfoot disturbed us?'

'Yes. What about it?'

'You dropped the flaming bags, that's what about it! The notes must have fallen out and you never even noticed, you steaming great twerp!'

'Now hang on, Baz. You were there too and you didn't notice either.' Nick was getting worried about the menacing tone in Baz's voice.

'Don't you try to blame me, you peanut-brain! It was your job to look after the money and you blew it! Why I ever took you along I'll never know. All that trouble and effort I go to and what happens? I do you a favour and let you in on it and you go and leave most of the loot behind! I don't believe it!' and Baz gave vent to his feelings by kicking Nick's pile of coins to the far side of the room. Nick stood speechless, not daring to move or say anything in case Baz decided to use his boots on him.

'Well, what are you standing there for?'

Nick started. 'What do you mean?'

'Come on. If the money's there, then it must be still there – no one goes in at the weekend. We can get it back with any luck. And you can do all the climbing this time, seeing as how it's your fault!'

They hurried to the car outside and Nick was too relieved at escaping Baz's vengeance to bother arguing.

'There you are, Bob. Everything just as it should be. The lad did lock it all up, just as he was supposed to.'

'Well, it's very strange, Mr Jenkins, very strange.' Bob puzzled it over in his ponderous way.

Fred Jenkins smiled tolerantly. He was used to Bob's slow-thinking ways. 'What's strange, Bob?' he prompted.

'But it was wide open – and there was nobody here!' he blurted out.

'It was wrong of the lad to leave it open like that,' agreed Fred. 'But no harm done, I dare say. Tell you what,' he said, seeing that Bob now looked and felt rather foolish, 'we'll take a look around, just to be on the safe side.'

Bob's face brightened and Fred knew he had made the right decision. After all, he thought, Bob was acting in good faith. It won't do any harm to humour him. He unlocked the gate and together they entered the yard.

'Seems all right, don't it?' said Bob.

'Yes,' agreed Fred. 'No one's here.' His eyes panned around the yard then paused and suddenly narrowed. 'Hang on a minute!' He walked towards the broken office door, suspicion hardened to certainty. He entered the building, Bob close behind, and at the threshold of his own inner office he let out a long low whistle.

'Well I'll be durned!' said Bob when he saw it. 'So I was right after all,' he added as an afterthought. Fred didn't reply, standing appalled at the chaotic mess before him, and failed to hear Bob's next comment.

'Sorry, what did you say, Bob?'

'I said "We'd better phone the police",' and Bob walked towards the phone on Fred Jenkins' own desk.

Fred came to his senses at last. 'No!' he shouted and

Bob stopped dead in his tracks, confused. 'No,' said Fred more gently. 'We mustn't touch anything, Bob.' He remembered the procedure; this was not the first time this had happened to him. 'The police will want everything left just as it is. I'll go and phone. You stay here in case anyone comes – and don't touch anything!'

With that he dashed off, leaving poor Bob bewildered but determined to carry out his boss' instructions, as he always had done.

Nick needed no further reminder from Baz that they were in a hurry. Baz's knuckles were turning white as they gripped the dashboard while Baz himself was leaning forward in his seat staring intently at the road ahead, even though they both knew the way like the back of their hand. Nick, too, was impatient to get there, to find out if the money was still there and get their hands on it again. After all the trouble and effort they'd gone to, to lose most of it through one stupid mistake was galling to say the least. All their dreams and plans would come to nothing if they couldn't find it, to say nothing of what Baz might do to him.

The corner of Lincoln Street was approaching fast. Nick slowed and changed down to third gear, taking the corner even so with a slight screech of tyres. His foot moved to accelerate towards their target. Suddenly it stopped, moved back and dug hard down on the brake pedal. The car screeched to an untidy halt and Nick stared disbelievingly down the street. Baz had seen it too, that ominous white and orange police car sitting right outside the entrance of the council depot. There could be little doubt why it was there. Nick couldn't believe their bad luck. Foiled just minutes before they could have got their hands back on the money. Baz saw the irony too and sat cursing at the sight before them.

Nick couldn't contain the frustration he felt and burst

out, 'I thought you said there'd be no one there at the weekend.'

'There isn't. I can't understand it.' Even Baz was short on explanations now.

'Well how come they discovered it so soon, then? There's cops crawling all over the place.'

'I don't know, do I?'

'You're the one with all the answers. What the heck are we going to do now? Breeze in there and say we're just looking for some money we dropped?'

'Don't try and be funny! If you hadn't dropped it in the first place we wouldn't be in this mess now.' Baz paused. 'Turn round and let's get out of here before they spot us.'

'And just leave the money there?'

'Well what else can we do?' Baz stormed at him. 'Go and confess? Turn this heap of yours round quick, or so help me I'll do some permanent damage to that ugly face of yours. Do I make myself clear?!!'

Abundantly clear, thought Nick as he performed a hasty three-point turn in the road and drove them away like two dogs with their tails between their legs.

'There! How's that?' beamed Jenny, as she put the finishing touches to the bunting draped round the walls of the old garage.

'That's fine, Jenny,' Liz smiled. She held the steps steady as Jenny climbed down and together they surveyed the scene. Bright red and blue paint dominated the abstract artwork that Liz and another art student had worked on all morning. Elsewhere the black walls of the garage were relieved by coloured light bulbs, posters, fish netting and the bunting which Jenny had just put in place. As the girls watched, the boys delegated to wire up the sound system demonstrated their success by turning on the music full blast. Simultaneously the various lights started flashing on and off, turning the garage into a home-made disco, full of life, light and sound. Everyone stopped working and enjoyed the effect, well rewarded for their day's hard work.

'Really cool!' Jenny gazed admiringly around the transformed garage. She turned to Liz. 'I bet the boys will be impressed when they see it tonight.'

'What boys?' said Liz without thinking.

'Oh, come on, Liz. Even you can't have forgotten those two fellers we picked up on the beach. Yours is really hunky but I think mine's sexier.'

'Oh, those two. I hadn't really thought about them.'

'Well, you've got to show some interest, Liz. Don't you want to have a good time this holiday?'

'But I am having a good time, and I thought you were too,' Liz blurted out.

'Well, yes, it's been fun today, but tonight's the real thing – this is just getting ready for it.'

'Yes, I know, Jenny, but don't you think you're getting a bit off-track? I mean, the whole reason for K Club is to tell people about Jesus, isn't it, not picking up boyfriends.'

'Oh, Liz, don't be such a stick-in-the-mud. Sure, I know this is a Christian thing and I'll do my bit, but there's no harm in enjoying ourselves too, is there? You do like boys, don't you?'

'Yes, of course, but I don't really think we've got time for relationships while we're on a beach mission.'

'Oh, don't be so old-fashioned, Liz. You don't have to ask a boy about his religious beliefs every time one of them asks you for a date!'

'Maybe not, Jenny, but I still don't want to get involved, especially not on this holiday and especially not with those two boys. I only invited them along here tonight because I thought they might be interested.'

'Oh they're interested all right,' winked Jenny. 'Yours

looked very taken with you.'

'That's not what I meant and you know it,' snapped Liz crossly.

Jenny giggled. 'I'll bet you'll be interested too before the night is out.' She dodged Liz's backhand swipe but knocked over a cup of coffee in the process. Liz had to laugh at her and they mopped up the mess together, their differences forgotten.

The opening night of the K Club started quietly. Word had not yet spread about the free coffee and few could believe that an old garage could house a decent disco. Only a few local youngsters had joined the K Club team and they were sitting nervously on orange boxes in one corner. The arrival of Al and Damian, rather overdressed but obviously street-wise, caused quite a stir, as it was designed to do. Jenny's eyes brightened, as she had begun to doubt they would come. She nudged Liz unnecessarily, for she had already noticed their arrival. Knowing that she had no excuse for ignoring them she reluctantly joined Jenny in welcoming them.

'Hi! Glad you could come,' said Jenny, flashing her wide smile at them both.

'Nice to see you,' was Liz's sincere attempt at a welcome. Ever since her last conversation with Jenny she was worried about Jenny's motives and could not relax easily now.

'Great place you've got here,' Damian enthused. 'You'd never guess from the outside. It looks really cosy.'

'Yes, we've been working hard on it all day. Haven't we, Liz?' Jenny couldn't disguise the pride in her voice as she turned to Liz. Liz smiled in return but said nothing.

Jenny persevered. 'It was Liz who did the mural. She's an art student!' Jenny was determined to impress the boys and make sure that Liz was friendly enough to

Damian so that she could develop her interest in Al. Damian was not slow to pick up the lead Jenny offered him.

'Really!' he said in admiration. 'I think it's great. Gives the place atmosphere. The colours are really striking.'

'Thank you,' Liz blushed. 'Are you interested in art?'

'Oh yes,' Damian lied. 'I like all kinds, especially modern art. What do you paint, mostly?'

Liz couldn't resist talking about her favourite subject and the next half hour passed pleasantly enough for all four of them. By half past nine a few more teenagers had drifted in and the place brightened up noticeably, the music and chatter vying with each other as the noise level increased. Both Al and Damian felt things were going really well and were annoyed when without warning the lights were raised, the music stopped and the intimate atmosphere was broken.

'What's happening? It's not throwing-out time yet, is it?' said Damian incredulously.

'No, it's just that one of our team is going to give a talk,' explained Liz, 'you know, about Christianity,' she finished lamely.

'Oh, fantastic!' Al exclaimed sarcastically and glanced darkly at Damian, as if to say 'I told you so.' But just then Daniel stood up to speak. His good looks gave him a very positive response from all the girls in the room while Al and Damian gave him only grudging attention.

Daniel spoke about a businessman, a jeweller who specialised in collecting precious gems so that his collection was admired and envied by other jewellers throughout the country. But still the jeweller wasn't satisfied, for none of his gems was truly priceless and although they gave him pleasure to look at, the pleasure soon faded and he had to buy others to keep himself amused and to make sure his collection was still the best. He yearned to own just one jewel that would eclipse all others, one unique gem which would satisfy him permanently so that he would not need any other jewels, for he would have the jewel of the world. For years he searched for the jewel of the world, buying various gems which he thought might suit, but always finding them lacking and losing interest in them. Until one day he found it – a pearl – the pearl of the world – and he knew it was what he had been searching for. The problem was it would cost a huge fortune, more than he owned. But because he wanted this one jewel so much, he went home and sold every other jewel he owned, even to his rival jewellers. He still hadn't enough, so he re-mortgaged his house and sold off all his other possessions. Finally he raised the money and bought the jewel. Although he was now bankrupt he was satisfied at last and considered himself the richest and most fortunate man in the world.

Daniel paused at the end of his story and the silence was electric. Everyone was aware that the story had a hidden meaning and was listening hard to have it explained. Even Damian found himself wanting to understand. Daniel knew he was the centre of attention but began to explain the story without a flicker of embarrassment.

'The businessman could be anybody, you or me. In fact, in a way he's everybody. The businessman collected jewels, surrounded himself with them in the hope that they would keep him happy. All of us do the same. We're all searching for happiness and most of us go on searching all our lives, surrounding ourselves with things: sports, a job, cars, hobbies, or the latest gadget, and still we're not happy. We're still looking for the one thing that will satisfy us, that will put everything in its rightful place because that one thing is in the number one spot in our lives. Well, the jeweller finally found it – the pearl of the world – and he sold everything to get it. Some others have also found this treasure, for it can be found by more than one person. Because the so-called pearl is not a jewel and it cannot be bought for money, for the pearl is . . .' Daniel paused to increase the suspense, '. . . a person,' he continued. 'His name is Jesus and he is free to everyone who seeks him, everyone who knows that money, possessions and the like will not ultimately satisfy them.'

Daniel changed the tone of his talk, explaining what Jesus meant to him and how people could get to know Jesus for themselves, but neither Damian nor Al were listening. Al snorted when the word Jesus was mentioned and dismissed the whole of Daniel's talk as religious nonsense. He now considered the whole set-up a con. He would have walked out if the thought of Jenny had not stopped him and he sat fidgeting crossly for the rest of the talk.

Damian too was deaf to the rest of what Daniel said but for a very different reason. Somehow, he couldn't explain why, every time the word money was mentioned, he inwardly jumped at the memory of what he had got himself involved in that morning. For he couldn't escape the feeling that he was implicated in the robbery. He had witnessed it, it was his own brother who had committed it, and to cap it all he had now hidden the evidence to protect his brother. What was Nick up to? He had no need to steal, surely. But then how did Damian know? How well did he know his brother? Maybe Nick was like the businessman in the story, always wanting more because he was dissatisfied. Come to think of it, was *he* any better? Would he have got involved in robbery if he'd had the opportunity like Nick did? He and Nick had nicked things from shops when they were younger. Maybe Nick had just never stopped. Damian shuddered and was uncomfortable for the rest of the evening.

Jenny was trying her hardest to placate a rather prickly

Al, whose earlier good mood had evaporated when Daniel's talk had confirmed his suspicion that the disco set-up was a front for those religious nuts to get their hooks into him. Still, Jenny didn't seem like that and had never mentioned Daniel's talk, nor anything religious. He decided to hang around a bit longer but make sure he met Jenny somewhere else next time.

'Do you want another drink, Al?' coaxed Jenny. 'Coffee's free, but the Cokes are twenty pence. I'll pay if you like.' Al seemed to be losing interest and she was desperately trying to recapture his attention.

'No, thanks. I think I've had enough.' Al didn't just mean the drinks. 'How about coming for a walk?' he said, standing up and making to leave, a sure signal for Jenny to follow if she was interested.

'I'd love to . . .' began Jenny, jumping up, when a warning tug from Liz pulled her up short. 'That is, I would love to but I've got to stay and help. We'll be packing up soon and we all have to help.' She didn't mention the prayer time at the end of each K Club evening which she would be expected to attend.

'Oh, suit yourself then!' snapped Al and turned to Damian. 'Coming mate? I've had enough of this hole!' Damian was startled out of his daydream by Al's abruptness. Jenny desperately looked for a chance to save the situation and show Al she was still interested.

'Look,' she flustered. 'I'm sorry we can't come tonight. House rules you know.' She laughed, embarrassed. 'But we can meet up tomorrow night. It's Sunday so there's no K Club. What are we doing tomorrow, Liz?' She turned to Liz for support.

Liz saw through Jenny's desperation and was again uneasy. On the other hand it had been a pleasant evening for her, more so than she would have admitted earlier and there seemed no harm in at least seeing the boys again. 'There's an open air service with the Salvation

Army on the prom at seven o'clock. We could meet you there,' she offered.

'What time does it finish?' Al's mood softened a little at this turn of events but no way was he going to be at anything religious again.

'About eight o'clock, I expect.'

'Right. We'll meet you down there at eight. See you,' and with that Al strode off abruptly, leaving Damian to smooth things over before he too left.

~ 7 ~

Sunday, 29th July

Sunday morning rarely existed in Damian's weekly schedule and today was no exception. After his disappointingly early night he had arrived home to watch the late night film and stayed up until the small hours. He emerged from his bedroom as usual at about midday and sat down to his mum's tasty roast dinner. Nick was there too and for the first time that weekend the family meal table was complete.

As he glanced across at his brother, Damian suddenly realised how their relationship had changed since Friday night. He was sitting facing a man with a guilty secret. Nick didn't seem any different, apart from being rather edgy. But Damian found it difficult to face him, knowing what he did about him. Should he confront Nick with what he knew? But what good would that do? Nick would only fly into one of his rages and would forever after be wondering if Damian would grass on him. No; Damian realised sadly that this one thing he would have to keep to himself. Just as Nick would keep his secret, Damian would have to keep his.

After lunch, he had to get out. His parents were settling down in front of the television again, probably to fall asleep later. Nick was there too, his presence too oppressive for Damian to stay any longer than he had to. He wandered into town to find something to pass the time, past the amusement arcade which held no attraction for him today. He sauntered on aimlessly and decided at last to walk to the lifeboat house and back. He wasn't usually keen on seaside strolls but the fresh air smelt good and he was enjoying the warm sun on his back and the sight of the holidaymakers on the beach was always a pleasant distraction.

He recognised too from a fair distance the beach pulpit which he and Al had helped build the day before. That brought back mixed memories! But the platform was now a focal point for dozens of adults and children, clustered around the edge of the prom or sitting cross-legged on the stones gazing up at the man on the platform waving his hands about.

As he approached, Damian heard the children singing and couldn't help a patronising smile at the scene. He slowed down and although he could have threaded his way through the adult crowd standing on the prom, he shuffled to a halt and watched the proceedings for a while. He was aware that Liz and Jenny would be here somewhere but he was enjoying the drama that was now being performed and the fast pace of the action held his attention for several minutes, as it had done for several other passers-by.

The drama finished and yet another person popped up from behind the platform. This was almost like Punch and Judy, thought Damian, and grinned at his own joke, until he realised someone might see him enjoying a children's entertainment and he sheepishly pretended to cough to hide his embarrassment. This latest figure was holding some colourful and very artistic-looking pictures as visual aids for his story; Damian wondered if they were Liz's handiwork. Normally he liked to show off to girls and hated being threatened by any accomplishments they had, but somehow Liz was different and even though he'd only met her twenty-four hours ago he felt he respected her and liked what he felt.

The man on the platform was explaining his pictures and made the story come alive with them. Each one followed the last in quick succession and the audience was swept along in imagination through each stage of the story's progress. Damian was only half listening to the words, preferring to enjoy the pictures and absorb the scene before him. Then the story-teller stopped, put down his pictures, paused, and continued in a much more assertive tone to the people before him.

'And Jesus said to the man, "You've only got one more thing to do if you want to get to heaven. Sell all the things you own, your house, your horses and all your fine possessions. Collect the money together and give it all away to the poor; then I know you are fit to be one of my followers." You see,' continued the story-teller, 'that young man was rich and loved his money. He'd probably spent all his teenage years building up his fortune and getting more and more money. He'd got to the point where money was the most important thing in his life. And Jesus won't allow anything to be more important than him in a person's life, not if that person wants to know Jesus personally.'

The young man continued but Damian heard no more; he felt dazed. Twice now someone at this beach mission had been talking about money. The very thought of it made Damian feel nervous now that he had his and Nick's guilty secret to protect, but to hear it mentioned in public gave him the jitters. Mind you, he couldn't imagine what was wrong with the rich man in the story. This Jesus fellow must have been very choosy about who he picked if this one failed the grade. And if you had to give away all your money to be a Christian that seemed daft too. Won't catch me doing that! he said to himself. After all, although Nick was way out of line, we're all out for what we can get, and I aim to get as much money as I can, he thought defiantly.

Still, the nagging feeling at the back of his mind wouldn't go away. How could anyone match up to God's standards if that was what he expected? There was no hope if God demanded that much from him and it was with a tinge of sadness that he turned away as the meeting came to a close.

Just then an elbow dug him in the ribs and Damian turned in surprise to find Al standing beside him. 'What you doing here, then? Going all religious, are we?' said Al, gently mocking.

Damian blushed but recovered quickly. 'Might ask you the same question,' he countered defiantly. 'You're the one who said you wouldn't be seen dead at a religious meeting again.'

'Dead right, and I won't. But that's not what brought me here. Look over there,' and Al nodded towards two uniformed policemen and another man who were making their way down the beach to the pulpit. Al was only one of a crowd who were now gawping curiously at the proceedings. The plain clothes man was obviously in charge and having found Tim, the Mission Leader, was speaking to him in an authoritative way. Tim was listening politely, and though no one could hear what was said, his face was going whiter by the second. Once or twice he appeared to protest and dispute what the policeman was saying but the man persisted calmly. By this time the whole of the Mission Team had realised what was happening and had gathered a few yards away. When Tim turned he took little time in picking out Graham from the group. Graham came to stand beside Tim and after a few more words, during which Graham's face also drained of colour, all five men moved purposefully to the waiting police car. The car's engine whirred into life and within seconds it had gone away in the direction it had come, leaving a wondering, gossiping crowd of bystanders.

'Well, what do you think of that, then?' said Al in mock horror. 'One of the God squad arrested for a dastardly crime. Shows they're just like us really, underneath,' he sneered.

'But that was Graham!' gasped Damian. 'You know, the one who was in charge of getting the pulpit down here yesterday.' He couldn't reconcile the cheerful, outgoing personality of the day before with the white-faced man who had just passed him.

'Oh yeah, so it was,' Al agreed. 'But so what! Doesn't make any difference. Probably killed his mother,' he joked cynically.

'Oh shut up and don't talk so wet!' snapped Damian and stormed off angrily.

Damian had more than one reason to be in a bad mood that afternoon. Graham's arrest was only a joke to Al. But Damian had other nagging thoughts in the back of his mind as to the reason for the police visit. Of course, Graham had nothing to do with the robbery, Damian knew that – but did the police? How on earth they imagined such a friendly, open guy like Graham could be a burglar Damian couldn't begin to guess. But he was at the council depot on Saturday and there was definitely a robbery there on Friday night, as Damian well knew.

For the rest of that afternoon he tormented himself with all the possibilities of what could be happening. Time passed agonisingly slowly and he toyed with the idea of asking at Green Shutters or even the police station. But that would have been a dead giveaway, he knew, so there was nothing to do but wait. When the time came for his date with Liz, Jenny and Al it was with more of a sense of relief than of excited anticipation that he made his way down to the prom.

'Didn't know if you'd be coming!' was Al's surly greeting when he saw him.

'Why shouldn't I?'

'Well, you seemed in a right mood this afternoon when I made that joke about our friend from the pulpit removal gang. Didn't know whether you'd lost your sense of humour or gone all soft and religious.'

'Stop talking daft. Your joke was in bad taste, that's all. It doesn't change anything else.' Damian tried to sound flippant. 'Besides we don't want to miss out on our date, do we?'

Al grinned. That was more like the Damian he knew. As they joined the crowd on the prom, Al just hoped Damian wouldn't try to swop partners and muscle in on his girl – it wouldn't be the first time. But Al intended to fight to keep Jenny. Jenny was stunning, a gorgeous blonde who was obviously eager for a holiday fling, while her friend Liz, though pretty, was more serious-minded and less interested in romance.

They caught the end of the last hymn from the Salvation Army band as they jostled among the onlookers at the back of the service. For a few seconds the music and singing mingled harmoniously with the distant surf splashing on the pebbles and the setting sun behind them played with the waves in endless patterns of light. Time seemed to stand still for a moment. Then, the service ended, the crowd turned and wandered away so that Damian and Al found themselves swimming against the stream like two rocks in a river.

'There they are!' cried Al after a minute or two as he spotted Liz and Jenny near the front of the service. 'Hi there!' he called and the girls looked up to greet them, Jenny's warm smile welcoming them both, Liz's face a mixture of pleasure and apprehension.

'Hi yourself!' returned Jenny to Al. 'What did you think of the Sally Army then? The hymns were a bit dreary, weren't they?'

'Ssh! Keep your voice down, Jenny,' hissed Liz. 'That's hardly the most tactful thing to say right here.'

'Oh, so what! I don't care who knows what I think,' Jenny retorted. 'It was dull and boring. Our Beach Special had far more life in it.'

Liz glanced nervously round to see who might be watching and listening. She wasn't sure that this second date was a good idea. 'Look, why don't we take a walk,' she ventured. 'I think we'd be a lot less conspicuous if we moved away from here.'

She glanced meaningfully at Jenny but her hidden meaning was lost on the other girl. 'Yes, let's,' Jenny responded. 'And can we find something to eat? I'm starving!'

The boys were quick to take the hint. 'How about some hot dogs?' offered Damian.

'Yeah! The best stall is Tony's,' Al added.

'OK. Lead the way, Al,' laughed Jenny and linking arms with her new boyfriend she let him take her off, laughing and joking, to Tony's hot dog stall.

'Hungry?' smiled Damian to Liz.

'Not really,' she laughed, 'But I'll let you buy me one if you're offering. We'd better join them anyway before they get into mischief.'

They followed the others, Liz keeping her distance from Damian, forcing him to keep talking. 'She certainly is a livewire, your friend, but I like her. That is, I like you too, of course. I like you both,' he flustered. Liz smiled at his confusion and Damian found himself blushing. He, the Casanova of so many holiday romances, actually found himself redden. This girl had made him feel uncomfortable, something few others had done.

Why couldn't she be like Jenny, put her arm in his and show him she was out for a good time too, instead of just standing there, smiling at him?

But Liz made no such friendly advances. She chatted and smiled comfortably at him as they queued, enjoying the sausage and onion aroma that wafted over them. Damian found himself beginning to listen, something he rarely did with girls. It was a novel experience but one he found he enjoyed once he stopped trying to impress Liz. He found out all about her home, her parents and brothers, their opposition to her coming to Shelham and her feelings towards them, her reasons for joining a beach mission and her hopes for a career in commercial art. He found himself sharing, too, not the bravado of the macho image he usually projected but something of the real Damian, his enjoyment of his job and hopes of moving to the big city soon to earn higher wages.

By this time they had left Tony's and were enjoying their supper walking along under the coloured lights of the prom while the noise of the crowds receded and the gentle surge of the sea provided a peaceful background to their talk. Suddenly Damian's ears pricked up at what Jenny was saying. Of course! Graham and the police! He must know what happened.

'It caused quite a stir, I can tell you. Green Shutters is positively buzzing with excitement. We've not talked about anything else all day.' Jenny was enjoying spreading the gossip and being the centre of attention. Never mind if she was exaggerating somewhat.

'That's hardly fair, Jenny.' Liz was cross at Jenny's misinterpretation of events, especially in front of outsiders, even if they were friends. 'We're not excited, just concerned for Graham – and the reason we've talked of little else is because his arrest could affect the whole mission this year.'

'Oh I don't know. It might draw more crowds – all

coming to see who's going to be arrested next – arsonists, thugs, murderers, who knows?' Jenny was being flippant but she didn't care, no matter how many dark looks Liz gave her.

Damian was getting increasingly frustrated at Jenny's inane chatter. 'Will someone please tell us what exactly has been going on?' he demanded with an edge to his voice.

'Yes, I will,' said Liz calmly, glad to set the record straight. 'It seems that the police suspected Graham of being involved in a burglary at the council depot yesterday. Apparently the office safe there contained a lot of money which was stolen some time over the weekend. And Graham was at the depot yesterday morning.'

'But that doesn't mean Graham did it,' Damian blurted out. 'It's preposterous!'

'Yes, I know,' Liz continued, 'that's what we all think. But apparently they found some unidentified fingerprints on the office telephone and when they asked the depot manager about it – he was the one who discovered the theft – he said that he had lent the depot keys to Graham on Friday night.'

'But he couldn't have stolen anything yesterday,' Al pointed out. 'He had no chance – we were with him all the time.'

'Yes, I know. He and Tim pointed that out to the police. But a council worker saw the gates open later in the afternoon and reported it to the manager. The manager told the police something else too, that when Graham returned the keys yesterday evening, he was acting suspiciously, very tense and nervous. The police thought that was grounds enough, which is why they arrived on the beach this afternoon.'

'But you haven't told the best bit, Liz,' broke in Jenny, as she took up the story. 'When we arrived back at Green Shutters from the beach there was another police car outside and a constable guarding the door!'

'Not only that, there were two detectives inside, ransacking the whole house,' added Liz.

'That's right!' said Jenny, enjoying herself again. 'Kate had to let them in – she was the only one left in this afternoon. They went through all our bedrooms, obviously looking for the stolen money. And they kept us in the garden for half an hour before they let us in!'

'Did they find anything?' said Damian, though he already knew the answer to that one.

'No,' said Liz, 'which is probably why they released him.'

'You mean they haven't kept him under lock and key in their cells, and fed him on bread and water?' Al sounded disappointed and Jenny giggled, elbowing him in the ribs.

Liz ignored them. 'No, they let him go this evening, but gave Tim strict instructions that he was to be responsible for him and that Graham mustn't leave Shelham.'

'So he's in the clear,' Damian felt very relieved, though the others could not have guessed how much.

'Not quite. You see, they've matched Graham's fingerprints with the ones on the office telephone,' Liz ended, and for once Jenny and Al had nothing funny to say.

There was an awkward silence between the four of them as they continued to walk in the gathering gloom. Jenny and Al were now walking hand in hand and showing that they would rather be on their own. Damian was devastated by Liz's revelations and could not bring himself to exchange small-talk with her.

The police still thought Graham was guilty and presumably might re-arrest him at any time. And all along Damian knew who was really guilty – Nick and the other man – but couldn't tell the truth out of loyalty to his brother. He felt wretched. Liz noticed his quietness but was too concerned over Graham to wonder about Damian. They might perhaps have walked for hours but they reached the headland where the cliffs jutted out into the incoming tide, forcing them either to retrace their steps or take the steep path to the golf links.

Liz spoke first. 'Well I suppose we'd better be heading back.'

'But why? It's only nine-thirty,' objected Al. 'You can't end a date this early, can you, Daim?'

But Damian didn't give Al the support he wanted and said nothing, allowing Liz to continue. 'I'm sorry, but we have to be up early in the morning. We're not exactly on holiday, you know, and I think we're going to be pretty tired this week, if the first two days are anything to go by. It's been a lovely walk but we must say good-night,' she said firmly. 'Coming, Jenny?'

But Jenny thought differently. 'You go on back if you want to, but I'm happy to stay out longer, if Al wants me to,' she declared.

Liz didn't like this, but realised that she had created this situation and couldn't get out of it. If Jenny wanted to have her holiday 'fling' with Al, there was little that Liz could do to stop her. She gave in as graciously as she could.

'All right, if you must. But I'm going back. I shouldn't be too late if I were you,' she added as a final warning. She turned to Damian. 'Would you mind walking me home?'

Al chose to misinterpret Liz's words and nudged Damian. 'Go for it, Daim!' he chortled and still chuckling he led Jenny up the cliff path, his arm around her waist.

Damian grinned, first at Al and Jenny, then down at Liz. He knew that he had been less than masterful so far, especially since the news about Graham. Normally he would have been terrified that his macho image might have slipped and done his utmost to restore his reputation. Somehow with Liz he found he didn't want or need to; it probably wouldn't have worked with her anyway.

'Come on, then,' was all he said and offering her his hand, which she accepted, led her back the way they had come. Now it was Liz's turn to be uncommunicative and Damian had to try to make small talk.

Finally she blurted out, 'I'm worried about Jenny. Do you think she'll be all right?'

Damian snorted. 'Don't worry about her. Al can take care of himself – and her!'

'I didn't mean like that! I just hope she doesn't get too involved. I don't think I trust Al.' To Liz's surprise the only answer she got from Damian was an uncontrolled fit of laughter. 'What have I said that's so funny?' she finally said, annoyed and perplexed by his unsympathetic reaction.

'I'm sorry Liz,' Damian chortled. 'It's just that people normally think I'm the one who shouldn't be allowed near girls. No one's ever said that about Al before, and you sounded so square – just like my old woman!'

'Oh!' Liz felt deflated by this unflattering remark and for the first time in their brief relationship began to feel she wasn't in control. 'So you're the one with a reputation, are you? Why haven't you tried anything on with me, then? Aren't I pretty enough?' Despite her principles Liz couldn't help fishing for compliments.

'Haven't really thought about it – I mean,' he added hastily, noticing Liz's darkening face, 'you're a bit different, that's all, not like all the other girls. I like you – a lot,' he ended lamely.

'Oh!' Now Liz wished she hadn't asked. She had better put things straight before this got out of hand. 'Look Damian, I'm glad we get on well together, and I like you too, but not in the way I think you mean. Our meeting on the beach and at K Club – it's just part of our job.'

'What!' Damian exploded. 'You mean you're just being friendly to us to earn your wages or something? Thanks very much!' He stuck both hands deep in his pockets and would not look her in the face.

'No, it's not like that at all! Oh dear! I'm not explaining this very well.' Liz put her hand on his arm and made him turn to look at her. 'I like you, Damian. I enjoy meeting you and lots of other new people here at Shelham. But I haven't come here just to enjoy myself or find myself a boyfriend for the summer. I came here, like all the others on the mission, to tell children and people our age' – she searched for the right words – 'well, to tell them about Jesus, really. We're all Christians, you see, and sharing our faith is very important – Jesus said so – and that's why we're all here. Jesus means more to me than anything else. I gave up the chance to earn a lot of money to come here and I want to do the best I can.' As Liz talked, her embarrassment had evaporated and her simple, peaceful manner was having its effect on Damian, who now stood listening intently, though he wouldn't look her in the face. 'So that doesn't leave much time for getting involved with you, does it? Sorry. Can we still be friends?'

There was only a grunt for an answer but he held out his hand again. Liz took it and they finished the journey back to Green Shutters, where he left her at the gate without saying a word. Liz entered the house feeling dejected. She had failed in her first real attempt at witnessing to someone her own age and made an attractive young man into an enemy, not a friend. Damian on the other hand had even more to brood on now. Yet again money had been mentioned – this time by someone who had sacrificed it in order to work for this Jesus. He was impressed by her dedication. But where did that leave him and Nick? How could Jesus mean more to anyone than money anyway? Money was the most important thing in the world, wasn't it?

It was much later that night when a solitary female figure walked down Augustine Street to Green Shutters. Jenny had insisted that Al leave her at the end of the road for even she did not want to face anyone at such a late hour. She looked at her watch again and almost broke into a run when she realised just how much she and Al had been oblivious of the time. She hoped that the Green Shutters door was still unlocked; to be locked out would be so embarrassing. All she wanted now was to creep in unobserved and go to bed.

She and Al had spent far too long at the golf links, she knew that now. But it had been such fun, at least to begin with. She had enjoyed the excitement of it all – the flattery of Al's romantic advances with the danger of being discovered adding an extra dimension to the sparkle of the escapade. But now as Jenny made her breathless way back to Green Shutters the sparkle had gone flat, like champagne left uncorked. By the time she had realised that Al's advances had gone too far, what should have been the best part of the evening had become an anti-climax and all she was left with was an empty feeling and a nagging sense of guilt which she couldn't get rid of. Jenny wished she had listened to Liz now, but it was too late for that. Maybe if she could just crawl into bed and the sleep of forgetfulness, the morning would make it all seem like a bad dream.

But as Jenny opened the kitchen door (thank goodness it was still unlocked!) she noticed a light on in the dining room. Was someone still up? She peered through the doorway and her heart sank. There, quietly talking, were the last people she wanted to meet now – Tim and Ann. She flinched at the prospect of having to explain herself to the Mission leaders, but what else could she do? Sleep outside in the garden?

The only way was to brazen it out – maybe they wouldn't say anything and didn't realise she'd been out all this time. She quietly entered the dining room.

'Hello, Jenny. I was wondering where you'd got to. Do you know what time it is?' Ann spoke calmly and quietly.

So they did know and she would have to face the music. Here goes, she thought. Aloud she said, 'Yes, I'm ever so sorry, Ann. I just completely forgot.'

'We were getting worried about you. Liz said you were with a friend you'd met at K Club, but you being this late anything might have happened.'

'I'm sorry you were worried, but there was no need. I can look after myself, you know. Besides, I wasn't missing any of the activities, so surely I can do what I like in my own time.' Jenny hoped she sounded casual enough to be convincing because inwardly she was a quivering mass of nerve endings.

Tim's face darkened. 'That's not really the point, Jenny. Perhaps it's time you and I had some plain speaking.' He motioned Jenny to a chair and with a sigh she dropped into it, her body glad to rest even though her nerves and emotions were stretched like a tightrope. 'We've been concerned about you, Jenny,' Tim continued, 'that's our job – to see that our team pulls together.'

'But that's not fair!' Jenny blurted out. 'I've done all you've asked me and been at all the meetings. Just because I stay out late one night you think I'm no good. You're biased against me just because I like to have a good time, not like those squares who've been coming here for years.'

'That's not true, Jenny, and what you've just said only deepens my concern. Now listen to me.' Tim took a deep breath before continuing, sending up a quick prayer as he did so. He told her of all the people he'd known on beach missions, all very different but all dedicated to sharing their faith with others and seeing young people become Christians. 'But you don't seem to share that vision, Jenny. Oh, sure, you go to the meetings and do all that's asked of you, but that's not the point. It's where your heart is, Jenny, – that's what counts. Mainly you've come here hoping for a good time for yourself. Am I right?'

For the first time he allowed Jenny to reply and although his last point hit home and she had to admit it was true, she couldn't help voicing a protest. 'But you're asking too much. I do my work, like you said, but I've a right to enjoy myself, to get some fun out of being here. What you want from me is too much for anyone to give.'

'It's not what *I* want, Jenny. It's what Jesus asks of you. He's not a hard taskmaster and you'll have fun, just like all the others do, but on his terms. Jesus wants your whole heart, Jenny; he isn't interested in anything less.'

'So I'm not good enough,' whispered Jenny.

'None of us is good enough, that's not the point. But you have got to make a decision, Jenny. If you're out to please yourself this fortnight, then it's best if you go home. But if you want to stay it's got to be on Jesus' terms, and that means you give everything to him and do everything for his sake, not yours. I'll give you twenty-four hours to think about it, then let me know what you've decided.'

Jenny sat unmoving, almost mesmerised, as she drank in Tim's words. She was unaware that Ann had risen, locked the back door and turned out the lights, until she came back to her and gently touched her elbow. 'Come on. Bed. We all need it. It'll be a long day tomorrow. Or should I say today?' Jenny rose unsteadily, trying to regain her poise but finding nothing to say. She climbed the stairs as in a trance and was barely able to return Tim's 'Goodnight!' It was with a subdued but deeply troubled spirit that Jenny finally sank into sleep that night.

~ 8 ~

Monday, 30th July

Jenny was not the only one to sleep restlessly that night. Damian had much to occupy his dreams as he tossed and turned. It was bad enough having to carry his brother's guilty secret without him even knowing, but now someone else was being blamed instead of Nick, someone whom Damian knew was completely innocent. Broken dreams haunted his sleep, dreams of Graham in handcuffs, Graham on trial, Graham behind bars, Graham crying out for help – then Graham and Liz pointing at him, accusing him; all of the mission, then all of Shelham staring at him, pointing their accusing fingers at him, Damian Everet, the one who sent an innocent man to prison. He woke suddenly in a cold sweat, to find sunlight streaming through his window and his mother waking him.

'Come on, lazybones. You're late this morning, your brother's having his breakfast already.'

'OK, Mum. Don't start nagging. I'm getting up.'

'Yeah. Looks like it!' said Mrs Everet with feeling. 'If you want any breakfast you'd better come down now.

But don't blame me if you're late for work', was her parting shot.

Blearily Damian entered the kitchen five minutes later just as Nick was finishing his toast and tea. 'Here he comes! The last of the world's great workers,' was his elder brother's sarcastic comment as Damian sagged on to a chair. He threw a snarl in Nick's direction but concentrated on drinking the steaming mug of tea in front of him. His hand seemed not to have the energy to lift the mug to his lips so his head compromised and met the mug half way. Gradually the tea had its effect on him and the drowsiness caused by his disturbed night disappeared. As the fog in his brain cleared he began to take in the image of his brother sitting opposite him. Nick seemed perfectly normal on the outside. Apart from being a bit touchy over the weekend, he seemed to be suffering no ill-effects from his criminal exploits and no trace of guilt shadowed his face. The irony was not lost on Damian that it was he, the innocent witness, who was suffering bad dreams rather than the burglar himself. He even wondered whether he had been mistaken in identifying his brother under the lamplight that night.

Nick broke in on his thoughts. 'Well, I can't sit here all day. Some of us have to work, you know!' and he pushed back his chair with a loud judder, grabbing his flask and sandwiches on his way to the back door. He resented the fact that Damian started work a half hour later than he did and lost no chance of reminding him.

'You'd better not be long, either,' Mrs Everet reminded him. 'You're not even dressed yet! What do you want for breakfast?'

'Not hungry!' was all Damian said and left the table as moodily as he had arrived, nearly colliding with his father in the hall and leaving his mother to stare wonderingly after him.

'What's eating him?' was Mr Everet's comment as he

sat down at the breakfast table.

'I don't know. They've been a right pair this weekend. As moody as a couple of love-sick girls.'

Mr Everet chuckled. 'I thought you told me boys were easier to handle than girls. They haven't had a sex change, have they?'

'No, you daft thing!' She smiled at his little joke. 'But sometimes I wonder if I know my own sons.' And with a shake of her head she turned to make her husband's breakfast.

Meanwhile Damian was puzzling over his predicament. Should he go to the police, tell what he knew and 'shop' his brother? No, he couldn't do that; whatever he might think of Nick he was still his brother. Or should he just forget about it all and leave Graham, and the Mission, including Liz, to suffer by being tainted with guilt in people's minds? People were quick to suspect and accuse, but slow to forgive or forget, at least in the world Damian knew. So although the latter course was the safest option, Damian found that the decision would not rest easy on his mind. Was it a new conscience he'd discovered in himself? Or just a fondness for Liz which prompted this unease? He didn't know. But if only there was something else he could do! He searched frantically for any solution.

As he left his bedroom he glanced through Nick's open bedroom doorway and on impulse turned his steps into the room. He looked round, half in anger, half in frustration. Why shouldn't Nick do something to solve his troubles? After all he was the cause of it all! Suddenly it came to him. Maybe Nick could help after all, even if he wasn't there. Maybe there was some clue somewhere in his bedroom, that might hold the key. Damian found himself looking hawkishly round the room, searching for – he didn't know what – but soon his hands and feet joined in the search as he ransacked the room. Drawers and cupboards flew open as his hands rummaged every-where. No luck. Nick was too clever to leave any evidence lying around. Damian sighed. He was already late for work. A last quick glance around the room, underneath the bed – and then he saw it. A slight bulge under the carpet right under the bed. He scrabbled underneath the old iron bed-frame, lifted up the tatty corner of faded brown carpet and pulled out his prize. Nick hadn't been so clever after all, for there, crumpled up in Damian's fist, were two official-looking blue cloth money bags. Not conclusive evidence, perhaps, but enough to give Damian something to think about and plan his next move. He quickly left Nick's room and re-hid the bags in his own bedroom. Now he had something to go on and he set off to work five minutes later with a more purposeful spring in his step.

Lunchtime in Shelham was no different to any other small town. Crowds and traffic increased as secretaries, shop assistants and workmen all made their way to buy or eat their midday meal. Pubs and snack bars became busier and noisier while others made use of their free time to shop for bargains or necessities. Shelham boasted no public park but those who preferred the open air made use of the many seats along Shelham prom.

It was here that Sandra joined the mingling crowd of lunchers and holidaymakers in the hope of meeting Baz at one of his usual haunts. He had not been at their usual meeting place, The Crown, and neither had he been there all day Sunday. She had sat there most of the evening on her own, trying to make her gin and tonic last and feeling very embarrassed by the looks and stares she was getting. Most of her girl friends saw little of her nowadays, for they regarded Baz as socially unacceptable and so found excuses not to meet her out of office hours. This had the effect of making her fiercely loyal to Baz, for the stubborn streak in her refused to accept that she was wrong and the others were right about Baz. This morning, though, her loyalty was stretched to the limit for she had not seen him since Saturday lunchtime and if she didn't know him better she would have said he was avoiding her. She had been aware for some time that he was in love with her, almost from the beginning, and it was that which kept her going through their stormy, unpromising relationship. If only he would settle down, find a steady job and become more an accepted part of society. But he had always been a rebel. Sandra knew this and accepted it, but her patience was wearing thin. She still wanted him, was even attracted by the rough unpredictability of his character, but would not stand for being ignored. Either he started paying her more attention, which included making plans for a holiday together, or she fully intended to give him the push.

She searched vainly in one amusement arcade after another, trying all the time to save her dignity by pretending to be just another casual tourist. She had almost given up hope when she spotted him by the whelk stall, indulging in his favourite sea food. He saw her almost simultaneously and rather sheepishly came across to her.

'Hello, Sand! What are you doing here?' he said, trying to look pleased to see her.

'Looking for you, of course. Where have you been?' she replied tartly.

'Look, I told you. I've got things to do. Don't question me like that. It makes me nervous.'

'But what's happened?' Sandra persisted. 'You were full of the joys on Saturday. Said you were going to book our holiday straight away, as soon as you could get to the travel agents.'

'Yeah, well, something's cropped up. We may have to postpone the holiday for a bit.'

'What?!!' Sandra nearly exploded and heads were

turned in their direction. Baz reacted swiftly and guided her away to where there were no inquisitive onlookers. But Sandra was not to be subdued. 'You told me it was all arranged. We discussed everything – a fortnight in glorious Crete – we even chose the hotel we wanted. And now you turn round and tell me we're not going! What kind of a man are you?!' she raged and barely kept herself from slapping Baz's unsuspecting face.

'Calm down, Sand and let me explain!' he pleaded. He continued quickly before she had time to burst out again. 'It's my latest business deal – it all went wrong Saturday afternoon. I was all set up, honest I was, and then my partner let me down – right berk he was – and I was left stranded. I should have netted a cool three thousand straight up, but all I got left with was a few hundred, hardly enough to cover my expenses.'

'I should have known, Barry Holmes, you and your business deals! You're all full of sweet promises but then you don't deliver the goods! When are you going to wake up and start living in the real world?'

'I'm sorry, Sand, really I am,' Baz whined and his pathetic face softened her a little. 'I'll try and get something sorted out soon, but I need a few days. OK?'

'Why don't we go somewhere else, then?' said Sandra in a more reasonable frame of mind. 'We could go somewhere less expensive and I could put my savings towards it.'

'No, I've told you before. If I take my girlfriend on holiday, I'm paying. I'm not having anyone say I'm your fancy man who sponges off all his women.'

'But who would know? Oh, give me strength! You men are all the same – on a permanent ego trip. You can't accept any favours from a woman, can you, in case it makes you look inadequate!' she taunted him, her scorn rising now to a pitch of fury. Baz positively wilted under her torrent of abuse, for once unable to persuade or cajole her. His sense of failure and frustration at himself was too great to deflect Sandra's well-aimed sarcasm. 'Well, you can keep your stupid pride and save your money. It's all off. I wouldn't go with you now anyway, not after this, not even if you got down on your knees and begged me!' She turned indignantly on her heel and stormed off, leaving Baz to face the embarrassing looks from passers by who had heard the tail-end of Sandra's abuse. He felt more desolate than he would have thought possible, the real prospect of losing Sandra now staring him in the face. She had threatened to leave him before, but he had always been able to calm her down, talk her round and make her forgive him and start again. This time, though, he was far from confident that he could do it again. She might cool down a bit later but Baz knew he'd need something concrete to convince her that he meant business and to win her back. He stood for a moment in deep thought, then slouched back along the prom hands deep in pockets, his mood black and unrelenting.

K Club was operating as normal that evening, at least as normal as was possible under the circumstances, thought Liz, as she gazed around at the faces of her fellow workers. Everyone was looking rather subdued at the moment, for the shock of Graham's 'arrest' had only partly subsided. The day's activities had carried on as usual and they had all put on cheerful faces as if nothing had happened, but it was as if a black cloud hung over them all. Tim had urged and encouraged them, reminding them that they were doing the Lord's work and not to let their feelings overrun them, but it was hard to stop yesterday's events stealing most of their joy and enthusiasm. They had all felt the shame as a family would and Liz realised for the first time how being a Christian really made you part of a huge family. The team members were from all parts of the country and many varied churches and backgrounds, but they all treated Graham as a brother in his trouble. So today had been lived out in a minor key, not helped when the police summoned Graham yet again for over an hour's questioning. Their continuing suspicion of him kept up the pressure on all of them during the day, leading to tiredness and irritability creeping up on some of the team. Liz would be glad when K Club finished and she could get to bed.

She was taken aback somewhat when a now familiar face appeared in the doorway as Damian entered the dim, cavern-like atmosphere. His eyes took a few moments to become accustomed to the gloom but when he saw Liz and Jenny he quickly made his way towards them.

'Hi! Fancy meeting you here. We can't go on meeting like this or people will talk.' They all laughed at his weak joke which really only emphasised the awkwardness between them. Liz was wishing he hadn't come, fearing a repeat of last night's scene with him. But it was Jenny he turned to first. 'Al is outside. He won't come in – says he doesn't want to be preached at – but he wants to see you. Will you go out and talk to him?'

Jenny gave a long sigh. 'I guess I'll have to, I can't avoid him.' She got up and smiled at Liz. 'Don't worry. I'll be all right.' She squeezed Liz's shoulder as she moved towards the door.

Damian's eyes followed her exit. 'She seems different,' he confided to Liz. 'What's happened to the good-time girl of last night?'

But Liz was not about to spill any secrets. 'Yes, she's changed a lot since yesterday. But you'd better ask her yourself. Come to think of it,' she continued, 'I didn't expect to see you here tonight.'

'Oh. Why not?'

Liz smiled thinly and shrugged her shoulders. 'Oh, I dunno. I suppose because of last night. I expect you thought I was too preachy. I didn't turn out the sort of girlfriend you wanted.' She was wishing this conversation wasn't taking place – it was becoming more embarrassing by the second.

But Damian laughed it off. 'Oh, don't you know? I'm the sort who always comes back. You can't put me off that easily.' He winked at her and Liz couldn't resist giggling at his mischievous grin. The mood between them immediately warmed and they began to chat amiably. Liz gave a silent prayer of thanks.

Outside the temperature was much cooler as Jenny tried to explain her reasons to Al.

'Look, I'm sorry Al, but the answer's no. I have a job to do here and I can't go off for walks just when I feel like it.'

'You didn't say that last night. You were very willing then, couldn't keep your hands off me!' Al was disgruntled by her change of tone and attitude.

'Yes, well, last night was last night and tonight is different.' Jenny blushed at the memory and was glad that Al couldn't see her confusion.

But Al persisted. 'Why? What's changed? I thought we had a good thing going for us.'

'It's difficult to explain, Al. Let's just say I've been doing some thinking. I'm trying to sort out my priorities and work out what I'm doing here and at the moment I just don't want to get too involved.'

'You mean I'm not religious enough for you!' said Al indignantly.

'No, it's not that. It's just that I've got to work a lot of things through and decide what's the most important thing in my life right now. Please understand,' she pleaded.

'Oh I understand all right!' sneered Al. 'Those religious nuts have got to you and are trying to turn you into a square, just like them. You and that stupid K Club.

They're a bunch of wets!'

'No, Al, it's not like that. Why don't you come and listen? Give them a chance.' But as she spoke, Jenny realised that was the wrong thing to say.

'Oh don't you start! You preachers really make me want to puke. Get lost!' Al strode off into the night, leaving a slightly tearful Jenny to re-enter the K Club alone. But behind her tears she knew that somehow she had crossed a divide and come down on the right side. Al's words had hurt her but with the hurt there was also a relief and a dawning sense of peace. Somewhere along the line she had made a decision and was only now aware of it. Tim's ultimatum to her last night had triggered off a whole lot of re-adjusting and coming to terms with herself. She didn't like what she had seen in herself but time and God would change that. At least she knew what answer to give Tim.

Inside the Club, Liz and Damian were enjoying the evening more than each had anticipated. Another team member, Ian, had joined them and soon had Damian talking about the subject he knew best – cars. It turned out that Ian was something of an amateur mechanic himself and was testing Damian's knowledge and enthusiasm. Jenny joined Liz who was listening fascinated to the two men talking animatedly about bits of metal she'd never heard of. Liz glanced up at Jenny, concerned for her friend. She knew something had gone on between Jenny and Tim the night before and had been praying furiously ever since breakfast when Jenny had told her a little of what she was going through. Now she longed to know how Jenny would react after seeing Al again. Jenny smiled again and reassured her. 'I told you it would be all right,' was her only comment.

Liz smiled with relief and turned her attention back to Ian and Damian's conversation. But at that moment, everyone's attention seemed focused on the doorway as

Jenny had been followed into K Club by Graham, who now stood talking with some other team members. He seemed calm and relaxed, smiling and sharing crisps and coffee with the group he had joined. Damian and Ian noticed too, and even stopped discussing carburettors long enough to comment.

'Graham looks cheerful enough, considering what he's gone through,' said Damian.

'Yes,' enthused Ian. 'He's been quite an inspiration to us really. In fact we're more upset about it than he seems to be. If it wasn't for him being so peaceful about it all, I think we'd all pack up and go home.'

'Don't be melodramatic, Ian,' Jenny corrected him. 'You know what Tim said to us all this morning. It's the Lord's work we're doing and that must come first whatever we're feeling like. None of us has the right to give up and go home just because something's gone wrong.'

'Yes, ma'am!' said Ian. 'I stand rebuked,' he said smiling. 'I didn't know you felt as strongly as Tim about it.'

'But Jenny's right,' agreed Liz, giving her an encouraging smile. 'We've got to trust the Lord to clear Graham in his own time, not worry about what other people think of him or us. Thanks, Jenny.'

Liz's words had a powerful effect. Jenny positively glowed in Liz's approval as they both realised that Jenny had at last shown her loyalty to the team. Damian too was impressed. Graham was obviously not allowing the scandal to destroy his peace of mind and others too were showing that they were quietly getting on with their jobs, doing what they believed in, finding strength from outside themselves.

I could never be like that, he thought ruefully to himself on his way home. They've definitely got something I haven't got. But how can I help get Graham out of this mess without involving Nick?

~ *9* ~

Tuesday, 31st July

This Tuesday was one of Damian's rare days off, agreed between the company and employees to compensate them for Saturday working. But despite being able to indulge himself in a lie-in, his mind refused to let him go back to sleep. The question that had been torturing him for the past two days just would not go away. Even now, when he had evidence of Nick's involvement in the robbery, he was no nearer the answer. What was he to do with the coin bags he'd found in Nick's bedroom? Drop them on the steps of the police station? What good would that do? Supposing he told the police he found the bags somewhere – that would lead to hosts of questions, and probably suspicion falling on him. Maybe that was the only solution – to confess to a robbery he didn't commit in order to spare someone else who didn't do it either. It sounded daft, but what else was he to do? It was too complex for him to work out – he desperately needed someone to turn to, but whom? Who would listen to his problems without wanting to give him a lecture like his parents? He needed someone who would understand and respect his confidence, not blab the secret out.

The answer hit him like an electric shock – Liz! Of course! She would understand and listen and give him good advice without preaching at him. He felt fairly sure of that, though he couldn't have explained why. But how to get her on her own? She was always with the other mission workers, and he could hardly ask her out on a date, not after Sunday night. But it was his day off. Maybe he could catch her on her own during the day, if he could just see her to arrange it.

He remembered someone saying last night that the Beach Special was at eleven. His watch said eight-thirty. Plenty of time yet. He rolled over and dozed for a while, his mind more at ease now that he had made a decision.

Eleven o'clock found him mingling again with the crowds at the back of the beach special. People will really think I've gone religious, all these meetings I keep going to, he mused wrily. It's a good thing Al's not here to see me. I'd never hear the end of it. Nevertheless he actually found himself enjoying hearing the children sing their action songs and answering the quiz with wild enthusiasm. There was a puppet display too which held the younger children spellbound. The speaker, someone Damian hadn't noticed before, was using the puppets to tell a story about a farmer who kept on extending his farm buildings to accommodate all his increasing livestock and show off his wealth. What's wrong with that? thought Damian. Though I can't see many farmers round here fitting that picture. They're always complaining how hard up they are.

The speaker was elaborating her story, making the puppets come alive as the farmer and his family and friends, until one night the farmer had a dream, more of a nightmare really, in which God appeared to him and spoke these terrible words. 'You fool! This very night you will have to give up your life; then who will get all these things you have kept for yourself?' The young woman went on to explain how Jesus was warning everyone not to live for money, piling up riches for themselves, when really they should be putting God first in their lives.

Damian felt conned. This was the third time he'd listened in at one of the mission meetings and each time someone was talking about money. If this was church, they'd pass round the collection plate now, he thought cynically. But somehow he knew that wasn't the speaker's motive. Indeed, although Damian didn't realise that the talk was one of a series that week on the theme of money, he got the definite idea that something or someone was getting at him. But to his surprise he didn't feel as resentful as he did at Sunday's talk. Maybe there is something in what she says, he thought. I suppose it is a bit daft to spend all your life doing nothing but making money. And if God is real, then I guess he's got to be more important than anything else in a person's life. Liz and Graham seem to be sure about putting God first. But that's no good for me. I've got more pressing problems to deal with. God can't help me with them!

He jerked himself out of his daydreaming as the last song was being sung and looked around to check where Liz was. He made a beeline for her as the meeting ended and was relieved to see that she didn't have children flocking round her like many of the workers did.

'Hello, Damian.' She seemed genuinely pleased to see him which made him return her open smile. 'I didn't expect to see you here. Not working today?'

'Day off,' explained Damian, then paused as he didn't know how to say what he wanted to ask her.

'Did you enjoy the Special?' Liz continued. 'Lydia's very good with those puppets, isn't she? But I don't suppose that's your cup of tea.' She faltered as she noticed

Damian's troubled and inattentive face.

'I've got to see you, Liz. On your own.' His bluntness told her he was in earnest.

'Well, OK. But I'll be busy until lunch-time. Is this afternoon any good? I take it this is something serious.'

'Yeah, it is. I need some advice.' Damian swallowed a lot of pride as he said this – asking advice – and from a girl too! Liz didn't seem shocked so he continued more confidently, 'Can you come round to my place – there'll be no one around and we can talk there.'

'Yes, if you like. But don't look so worried. I'm sure it's not as bad as all that.'

Damian forced a smile. 'Wait till you hear. Anyway its 13, Latimer Road. Two o'clock OK?' He wouldn't stay after that, despite all Liz's efforts to engage him in small talk and introduce him to other team members. He felt awkward among them now and was glad to escape to the refuge of The Fox to enjoy his lunch-time with Al and some of the other mechanics.

'Oi, Nick, over 'ere!'

Nick turned in surprise to see Baz beckoning him from across the street. He filtered out of the flow of pedestrians and weaved his way across the lunch-time traffic.

'Hello, Baz. What are you doing here? Come and join us for a pint,' he offered.

'No time for that!' snapped Baz. 'Where've you been? I've been waiting ages for you to come out.'

'We have to take it in turns in Stores. It's my week to have late lunch. Half past one! My stomach's rumbling!' Nick complained.

'Never mind that! I've got a little job on and you're gonna help me.'

'What! Don't talk daft! This is broad daylight, remember. Are you off your trolley?'

'Don't talk to me like that! And stop wasting time.

We haven't got long if you wanna get back to that precious job of yours!'

'Look, this is crazy!' Nick protested. 'Can't we at least talk about it?' He dug his heels into the pavement as Baz tried to drag him away. 'Stop it! I dunno what you're up to, Baz, but if you're doing a job right now in broad daylight, then count me out. I want no part of it. In my lunchtime too!' Nick was indignant.

'Now look, you wimp! You owe me! I haven't forgotten it was you who left the money behind in the depot Friday night. Now I'm short of dough because of you and I need some fast!'

'Why? What's all the hurry? You were always the one for planning things thoroughly, you told me,' Nick objected.

'Never you mind why!' Baz was in no mood to let Nick know that it was because of Sandra that he was desperate for money, and that this was his last-ditch attempt to win her back by paying for the holiday she so much wanted. He continued to pull Nick along with him until Nick resigned himself to missing his lunch hour and listened to Baz's plans.

'Now listen,' Baz ordered. 'A friend of mine has lent me some skeleton car keys just for today but he's gotta have them back by tonight or he loses his job. Now all we've gotta do is find the right car, with the right key and we're home and dry. I know a bloke in Dagenham who'll pay cash for any car, no questions asked. So come on. Stop dragging your feet and get a move on!'

'What do you want me for? Sounds like you've got it all sorted out,' Nick pointed out.

'I need you as lookout, stupid! And it looks less suspicious with two of us. Besides, if anything does go wrong, I've got you as an alibi, haven't I? But don't expect a 50–50 split on the money this time, cos the risk's all mine. You're just my assistant,' he crowed. 'But I might let you have a grand or so if you play your cards right.' Nick's face lifted at the mention of money, as Baz had calculated it would. 'Now come on. There should be some Rovers or Sierras down this way. Who knows? We might even find a nice BMW.'

Baz led the way hurriedly to the side road behind the top end of the High Street where most of the banks and estate agents were situated. Here he reckoned to find the classier cars parked. Nick tagged along, a reluctant partner, but overawed as usual by Baz's bullying and the lure of extra cash. Turning the corner they sauntered along the row of shining cars which contained, as Baz had predicted, several expensive models owned by the town's wealthier businessmen. Unfortunately Baz was less than expert at finding his way around the huge bunch of car keys he had borrowed and Nick winced with embarrassment at Baz's vain attempts to unlock the door of a brand new Golf Convertible.

'Someone's coming!' he hissed and Baz immediately straightened up and continued along the street. Nick had to admire his nerve. 'All right. Coast's clear,' he said and Baz started examining doors again. Suddenly the driver's door of a newish Rover Vitesse surrendered to Baz's grasp and the door swung open. It wasn't even locked! Grinning at his luck, Baz dived into the driver's seat and fumbled with the keys for the likeliest one to fit the ignition. Nick watched with bated breath as one key after another was rejected, both of them getting increasingly agitated at being so agonisingly near to success. Unfortunately Nick concentrated on Baz so much that he forgot his own purpose in being there and it was not until he heard the shout of indignation that he looked up and saw the car's owner crossing the street.

'Look out!' he cried, but before Baz could scramble clear, the irate man was upon them, his portly figure belying the speed with which he closed down on the would-be thieves of his beloved car. Brushing Nick aside he confronted Baz, still struggling to rise out of the car.

'And just what do you think you're doing, you young hooligan? I'll have the law on you!'

'Ah, shut up, grandpa!' Baz retorted. Unable to run, his temper got the better of him and he chose to brazen it out. He faced up to the man and tried to push past him.

The man was not going to let him off so easily. Unwisely thinking he could make a citizen's arrest on the red-handed car thief he grabbed Baz by the shoulder. 'You're coming with me, my lad!' were the last words he spoke.

He reckoned without Baz's brute strength and dirty-tricks fighting. Baz spat in his face, punched him in the stomach, twisted the hand on his shoulder round behind the man's back and shoved him head first into the nearest wall, all before Nick had time to even blink. The man crumpled in a heap and lay still.

For a few seconds no-one spoke. Nick was stunned in disbelief. Baz was breathing hard and rubbing his hands. Finally, Nick spoke up. 'You've killed him. You great berk! You've murdered him!'

'Don't talk wet!' was Baz's retort. 'He's only knocked out.' He quickly glanced up and down the lonely side street. 'Quick! Help me search his pockets before some-one comes.'

'Haven't you done enough for one day?' Nick was incredulous.

'Oh suit yourself, you stuffed dummy! You always were pretty useless.' Baz gave him an ugly look. 'Ah!' His face brightened. 'Here we are!' And he held up the man's car keys. 'The old bloke's done me a favour after all. Much easier with these. I'm off. I should clear off if I were you before someone sees you. And don't expect to see me for some time. Cheerio, chicken!'

And with that, he jumped into the car and drove off, fast, into the High Street traffic. Nick looked down at the fallen man, then up and down the street. A housewife was just emerging from a house at the far end. In blind panic he took to his heels and ran.

Liz was having second thoughts. She was fairly sure that Damian was on the level and really just wanted to talk, but on the other hand she recognised that it was not the done thing to go visiting a young man alone in his house, even if it was the middle of the day. Jenny had finally told her what had happened on Sunday night, especially her showdown with Tim, and Liz did not want the same treatment from the mission leader. In the end she decided to tell Tim and Ann over lunch and hope to win their approval.

Tim was thoughtful. 'I don't like it, Liz. You shouldn't have agreed to go to his house. And you know what mission policy is about counselling the opposite sex. But you say you've promised to go?' Liz nodded. 'Well, you'd better not break your word. But I'd rather you didn't go alone.'

'But I don't think he'll talk if anyone else is there,' Liz protested.

'Then he'll have to lump it,' Tim concluded with authority. 'But don't worry. If we send the right person with you, I'm sure he'll be tactful.' Tim paused, looking round the room at the various faces, then seemed to come to a decision. 'Graham, can I have a word?'

It was half an hour later that Liz knocked on the door of 13, Latimer Road, the broad figure of Graham beside her. It was certainly reassuring to have Graham there, for she didn't relish trying to advise Damian on her own and felt very vulnerable. Graham had been so understanding too, listening to the brief history of her relationship with Damian and offering helpful comments without once referring to his own personal dilemma. He really was an inspiration, Liz thought as she glanced back at him. Here he was, practically accused of a major robbery and yet quietly and patiently waiting for God to sort it out, with a deep faith that everything would work out for good in the end. Neither of them had any idea how soon that was going to happen.

Damian opened the door, but his smile on seeing Liz froze as he noticed Graham standing behind her. He held the door open for them both until they stood facing each other in the hall.

'I thought you were coming on your own,' he accused Liz, with the unspoken question, 'What's he doing here?'

'Yes, I know. I'm sorry, Damian, but Tim – he's our Mission Leader – wouldn't let me come alone.' She smiled, trying to win back his confidence. 'I guess you can blame it on Al and Jenny. After their little adventure on Sunday night, Tim's being ultra cautious.'

'Oh yeah,' Damian grinned back. 'Al's just told me about that. But it's you I wanted to talk to,' he said, looking very dubiously at Graham.

'Look, why don't we sit in the garden,' offered Graham, to break the tension. 'It's such a hot day – seems a pity to be stuck indoors.'

The idea was a brainwave and Liz tried to give Graham a grateful look as he and Damian set out the garden chairs. Graham sat discreetly a little apart as the others began their conversation.

Damian didn't know how to begin. Graham's presence had confused him as he was the very man he was trying to help. The conversation limped from one triviality to another and Liz was feeling more and more uncomfortable. She looked in desperation again to Graham, who took the hint. 'Why don't I go and make some drinks?' he offered and disappeared into the kitchen before the others could refuse.

Liz turned back to Damian. 'So what was really on your mind, Damian?'

Damian could contain himself no longer. There was no roundabout way of saying what he had to say. 'It's about the robbery,' he blurted out. 'I know Graham didn't do it.'

'Well, so do we all,' agreed Liz. 'Is that all you wanted to say?'

'Yes, I mean, no. You don't see, do you? I *know* he didn't do it, because I saw who did!'

The information dropped like a bombshell into Liz's brain and stunned her into silence. 'Well, why don't you go to the police, then?' was all she finally offered.

'Because I can't!'

'But that's stupid . . .' began Liz, then bit her tongue as she noticed his shocked expression. He wanted her help and advice and she wasn't making a very good start. 'I see,' she began again. 'Is it someone you know, someone you want to protect?' Damian's curt nod spoke volumes. Liz saw the hurt and anguish in his face and realised at last what all this was costing him. 'It must be very difficult for you,' she sympathised. After a pause she continued, 'Have you thought of facing him with it? Telling him you know and trying to persuade him to give himself up?'

'Hardly likely to do that, is he? And what if he threatens me?'

'Then you must go to the police,' Liz persisted. 'Or you'll end up in trouble too. And what about poor Graham?'

'Do you think I don't know!' Damian burst out angrily. 'It's knowing he's being blamed for it is giving me nightmares! But what can I do? I can't shop my own . . .' Damian swallowed the last word of the sentence, realising he'd nearly given away Nick's identity.

Liz had noticed his slip and was beginning to put two

and two together when they were both disturbed by the sound of running footsteps. A few seconds later the side gate opened and a distraught man burst into the garden, nearly colliding with Graham emerging from the kitchen with their drinks.

'Nick!' exclaimed Damian. 'What on earth's happened to you?'

'It's Baz!' Nick blurted out, between breathing great gulpfuls of air. 'He's gone and killed a man!'

'Calm down.' Graham's quietly authoritative tone took control. 'Tell us slowly what happened. Who is this Baz?'

'He's a friend of mine – well he was,' said Nick. 'He had this crazy scheme of nicking a car, but we got caught – the owner came back. There was a fight and Baz threw him into a wall. I reckon he's dead! Then Baz jumped in this bloke's car and drove off.'

'Is this Baz the one you did the robbery with on Friday night?' Damian interrupted.

Nick looked aghast at his brother. 'How did you know . . .?'

'Never mind that, now,' Graham broke in. 'Has an ambulance been called for this man?'

'There was a woman coming along the street. She must've found him,' explained Nick.

'Then we'd better phone the police. Or rather, you had, Nick,' Graham ordered. 'If this man is dead, then the sooner you go to the police and tell them what you know the better for you. Otherwise you could end up facing a murder charge.'

'Yeah, sure, anything you say,' agreed Nick, so panic-stricken that he would have jumped off a cliff if Graham had told him it would get him out of trouble. Graham found the local police number and dialled, then handed the receiver to Nick. He made a poor job of telling his story over the phone but eventually, with several promptings from the others, he got the sergeant to understand and agree to send round a police car for them.

'Well, that's that,' said Nick as he put the phone down. 'I'm to go down to the station and make a full statement. Might as well confess to the Lincoln Street job at the same time, I suppose.'

'I'm sure they won't be too hard on you,' said Liz. 'After all, you didn't hit the man, and this Baz was the leader in both robberies.'

'Yeah. He's the one they should be going after,' said Damian with feeling, angry on his brother's behalf. 'But I expect he's half way to London by now.'

The others commiserated but Nick was thoughtful. Suddenly he shouted. 'No! He isn't!'

The others looked perplexed. 'What do you mean?' said Graham.

'Of course!' said Nick, unhearing. 'He'll collect up all the loot first, plus all his other gear. That's too valuable to leave behind.'

'Nick!' exclaimed Damian. 'What are you talking about?'

Nick faced them all. 'I know where Baz is,' he announced, 'and if we're quick we can still catch him. He's up at the hideout on the Old Farms Road. Come on! Let's go before he gets away.'

'Aren't you forgetting something? The police will be here in a minute,' Liz pointed out.

'But if we wait we'll lose him,' Nick wailed, desperate now to catch the man who had ruined him.

Graham thought quickly. He had to come to a decision about Nick and somehow he felt he could trust him. 'OK,' he said. 'You three go on. Nick will show you where this hideout is. I'll stay and wait for the police.' With some protests from Liz he shooed them out of the door. 'But be careful!' were his parting words.

They jumbled into Nick's car and for once it started

first time. The rusty Escort bumped and battled round the bends and potholes of the minor roads Nick took to avoid the town centre and within five minutes they were climbing out of Shelham towards the distant derelict buildings which once housed a small farming community. The road surface deteriorated but Nick did not slacken speed. His hands gripped the steering wheel and he stared through the windscreen obsessed with his objective – catching Baz before he got away. Damian braced himself against the dashboard and tried to keep his rebellious stomach in order. Liz was desperately trying to stay upright in the back as the car swerved violently from side to side. Fortunately for her the journey itself stopped her thinking of the hazards ahead and panicking at the idea of chasing a run-away criminal. Afterwards she wondered how she ever managed what she did that afternoon.

'There's the car!' Nick suddenly shouted, though they saw it as soon as he did. The car screeched to a halt behind the white Rover and Nick and Damian shot out, Damian needlessly telling Liz to stay behind – for Liz had no intention of confronting the violent man inside. She cowered down in the back seat as the two brothers approached the ramshackle cottage.

Nick led the way inside and found Baz as he had expected in the room where less than a week ago they had first planned the burglary. Baz had heard them coming and stood aggressively in front of the fireplace, a crowbar in one hand. Nick hesitated, then slowly moved to one side of the doorway as Damian entered beside him.

Baz glared menacingly at them. 'I thought I'd seen the last of you,' he said coldly to Nick. 'And who's your friend?'

'It's no good, Baz!' Nick spluttered. 'I've talked to the police. They know everything.'

'What!' Baz eyes narrowed. 'You little grass! I warned you. I'll murder you for that!' and he advanced threateningly towards Nick.

'Hold it, mate! Don't you get violent with my brother or you'll have me to deal with as well.' This from Damian.

'Oh, so he's your brother, is he? Needs you to hold his hand, I suppose! Well that's what I'd expect from a chicken like him. But neither of you is gonna stop me, if I have to do you both in!'

'But it's no use, Baz! Don't you see?' pleaded Nick. 'It's gone too far! Thieving's one thing, but violence and – and – murder . . . You can't go on like that.'

'Oh can't I? We'll see about that. But I haven't got time to stand around listening to you preach morality at me. Are you gonna get out of my way or do I have to make you?'

'You ain't going nowhere, mate,' said Damian, threatening in his turn. 'We're all gonna stay right here until the police come.'

At Damian's words, Baz's expression contorted savagely and like a wild animal he sprang. With a fierce snarl he lashed out with the crowbar. Damian half expected the attack and was able to parry the blow but the heavy metal bar landed bruisingly on his upper arm, making him stagger and fall. Baz turned on Nick who gaped incredulously at the man who was once his best friend.

'Baz! What are you doing?' he asked, refusing to believe that the savage creature in front of him was the same Baz he'd shared so many laughs with. 'You can't . . .'

Without waiting to listen Baz hammered the crowbar down on Nick's unprotected head. Silently Nick collapsed like a scarecrow without its sticks, the astonished look still fixed on his features. Baz hesitated then, doubt and regret momentarily delaying his frenzied actions, so

118

that Damian, recovering on the other side of the room, had time to spring on to Baz's back and grapple him to the floor.

Outside, Liz was finding her initial terror mixed with curiosity as the seconds ticked by. She changed her mind about staying in the car, realising that it wasn't a safe place anyway if someone was to attack her and that she'd have more chance of running away out of the car. She climbed out of the back seat and drew nearer to the scene of the action. She began to hear voices from the house, then shouts and sounds of a scuffle. She ducked out of sight behind the Rover which Baz had stolen and as she did so her head came level with the steering wheel and her eyes fell on the car keys still dangling in the ignition. In his haste Baz had obviously not bothered to pocket them. With a coolness she afterwards marvelled at, Liz reached in and clasped the keys. She could still hear the struggle indoors and she puzzled furiously over what to do with her find. Her eyes searched around frantically, her mind fighting to think and act rationally while her whole body screamed at her to panic and run. Then she saw it, just the other side of some rubble, a long-neglected and weed-strewn duck pond – more of an overgrown puddle really, but ideal for Liz's purposes. She flung the keys far over the rubble and heard the gratifying plop as they hit the water.

Her satisfaction was short-lived, however, for the next sound was the noisy footsteps of someone leaving the house in a hurry. Ducking instinctively she crab-ran to the back of the Rover. Through the back windscreen she saw an unknown man appear and half-run, half-limp to the driver's door. Baz had shaken Damian off and was now leaving everything in his panic to escape before it was too late. He swung open the door, then froze. The keys were gone and he had noticed at once. He looked up and around furiously for whoever had thwarted him.

Panic rose up in Liz's throat. She wanted to scream as she backed slowly away from the danger a few feet in front of her.

Baz was facing the other way as she turned and prepared to run. But as she did so her foot scuffed a stone. Baz heard instantly and wheeling viciously on his one good heel he saw her and advanced. His menace nearly paralysed Liz with fear as she backed away in terror, held by his evil gaze like a rabbit by a snake's. His hand reached out towards her – then suddenly withdrew. He snarled in fury at her and turned away as she watched in disbelief. But now her ears began to pick up what he had already heard – the unmistakable, sweet welcome sound of an approaching police siren.

~ 10 ~

Wednesday, 1st August

Damian knocked at the wide door of Green Shutters at the pre-arranged time of one o'clock. Finding the door ajar he thought it safe to push it open and peer into the tiled hall, cluttered with pullovers and various personal belongings. No one had come in answer to his knock so he ventured inside. Just then, Tim came striding down the stairs.

'Ah, Damian! Glad you could make it.' They shook hands and Damian winced. 'Sorry,' Tim apologised. 'I forgot that's the arm that got hurt. How's your brother?'

'Not too bad, thanks. The doctors say he can go home tomorrow. I've just come from visiting him. He looks a right mess – covered in bandages. He had to have six stitches, too – feeling very sorry for himself, he is.'

'Poor man!' Tim commiserated. 'And how are your parents taking it?'

'They've gone potty. Mum's worrying like mad and keeps on asking Nick questions about it all and Dad just does nothing – sits there and hangs his head and won't even speak. I don't think they'll ever get over it – they look about ten years older.'

'Yes, it must be very hard for them,' agreed Tim. 'Anyway, you must be hungry. Come on through and have some lunch. Everyone's in the garden, in case you wondered why it was so quiet.'

The unusually hot day had drawn everyone to the back garden to enjoy their salads in the sunshine and Damian was soon made welcome in their midst, with a plate in his hand and a wall to sit against. Graham, Liz and several others moved over to join him, for news of the dramatic events had been almost the sole topic of conversation for nearly twenty four hours. Damian had to repeat his story a number of times and in increasing detail so that he took a long time to finish his lunch. But he found he quite enjoyed all the attention as he sensed that they were all genuinely concerned for his and Nick's welfare. Gradually people drifted away as the meal time ended and Damian sat quietly with Tim, Liz and Graham.

'By the way – thanks for all you did yesterday, Graham,' said Damian, 'you know – organising us all, – and everything,' he ended lamely. He wanted to say so much more, to apologise for all the trouble his family had brought on Graham and to offer tentative friendship to the man who had every right to regard him as an enemy. Fortunately Graham sensed Damian's embarrassment.

'No need to thank me,' he replied, smiling. 'I was only too glad to help. But I must admit I'm a bit sorry now to have missed out on the action. You three had all the excitement – all I did was tell the police where you were. They wouldn't even let me go with them.'

'I shouldn't worry. Thàt sort of excitement I can do without,' joked Liz. 'I've never been so frightened in all my life. When that man came for me I really thought he was going to kill me.' Liz remembered and shuddered.

'You're safe enough now,' Tim reassured her. 'The police have him and he won't come out for a very long time by the look of things. But if I had known what was going to happen this time yesterday I'd never have let you and Graham leave here.'

Damian began to feel uncomfortable again, realising what danger Graham and Liz had been in, and how the whole Mission had suffered – all because of his family. But Graham came to his rescue once again.

'All's well that ends well, Tim! You're beginning to show your age,' he teased. 'I wouldn't have missed the past few days for anything. It's taught me so much about trusting the Lord and not worrying about things that are out of my control. But we ought to be grateful to you, Damian. It must have been very hard on you, knowing that your own brother committed that robbery and that I'd been accused of it. I certainly appreciate what you tried to do to get me out of trouble.'

Damian was speechless at Graham's generosity in thanking him instead of blaming him as he deserved. A smile spread over his face and a warm glow spread through him. He was totally accepted by these new friends of his, despite all his shortcomings. He turned to Liz and found her smiling back at him as if she guessed what was going through his mind.

They were interrupted by the arrival of Shelham's police inspector, shown through the garden by Daniel. Tim rose to meet him, followed by the others.

'Good afternoon, Inspector. Can I offer you some lunch?' offered Tim.

'No thank you. I'm still on duty. This is a courtesy call really, to put you in the picture, so to speak, about recent events.' Then he spotted Damian. 'Ah, but I see you have company. No doubt this young man has been telling you all you need to know,' he grinned.

'No, I haven't!' retorted Damian. 'I don't even know myself. You haven't even told us what will happen to Nick.'

'Hold on a minute, son, and calm down,' countered the inspector. 'Your parents have been informed just now, but you weren't with them of course. Your brother is technically under arrest for burglary but in view of his injuries and his assistance in the capture and arrest of Holmes, he will be allowed to recuperate at home, where your parents have agreed to vouch for his good behaviour. He'll have to come down to the station to make a full statement, of course, and he'll appear in court to face charges next week, but I'm glad to say there'll be no objection to bail and he'll be free to return home until the trial in a few months' time. Hopefully the judge won't be too hard on him as it's his first offence and he did assist the police with their enquiries,' he smiled.

'And what about Holmes?' asked Tim.

'No bail for him, I'm afraid,' said the inspector grimly. 'Not after his violent behaviour, and his threats against your brother. But they've both confessed, so the trial will be straightforward and we won't need to involve any witnesses or innocent bystanders.' Here he turned to Graham and Liz with an apologetic smile and the significance of his gesture to Graham was seen and accepted by them all.

'Will he be tried for murder as well?' Liz wanted to know.

'Murder?' said the astonished inspector. 'GBH certainly, as well as theft and criminal damage . . . . . .'

'But what about the old man?' interrupted Graham, 'The owner of the car. Nick told us that Barry Holmes had killed him.'

'No, he didn't, fortunately,' said the inspector solemnly. 'Cracked his skull, though, and he's under close observation in hospital. But he'll be all right in a few days.'

'Thank goodness for that!' sighed Liz, and the relief all round was obvious.

'Well, I must be on my way,' said the inspector. He turned to go, then checked himself. 'There's just one curious thing,' he said, sharing his puzzlement with the others. 'The stolen money. We've only recovered about a third of the money, all in coins. The men swear that's all they took – say they left the rest behind – but we haven't found a trace of the money anywhere. We've searched the depot thoroughly too.'

As the inspector was speaking, Damian felt himself go redder and redder. He'd forgotten all about the rolls of banknotes! Why didn't he say something about it yesterday? He'd be in trouble himself now. Still, there was no getting out of it now. He'd just have to face the consequences.

'Er, excuse me,' he stumbled. 'I think I can help you there.' Four pairs of eyes swivelled round to him, making him even more conscious of his predicament. 'I can show you where it is.' The inspector's eyes lit up. Damian turned to the others. 'I'm sorry to spoil a beautiful friendship,' he said, 'but I'm afraid I'm going to have to ruin your beach pulpit.'

'You see,' said Damian to Tim half an hour later as they surveyed the wreckage of the sandy structure, 'I had no idea which sandbag it was in!'

The inspector had lost no time in organising his constables with shovels and ferrying them all down to the beach. The rest of the mission team had followed in hot pursuit, realising that some more excitement was about to begin and determined this time not to miss it. To the amusement of all the holidaymakers watching, the constables had knocked down the artistic sand facade of the pulpit and dug out each sandbag in turn. Cries of 'Shame!' and 'Why don't you build your own sand-castles?' from various wags in the crowd had enlivened the entertainment for all until even Tim could see the funny side of the destruction of his beloved pulpit.

It was the tenth sandbag. As the constables poured out the sand once more in their messy task, out fell three decidedly soggy bundles of papers, dirty but still recognisable as a mixture of five, ten and twenty pound bank notes.

'Aha!' beamed the inspector as he pounced on his prize. 'This must be it!' He turned to Damian. 'Well done, lad! Full marks for initiative, though your hiding place was rather unorthodox and you should really have handed it in to us. But I know your motives were good and it certainly stopped it falling into the wrong hands.'

For the second time in an hour Damian was speechless. Did the inspector really believe he hid the money to stop Nick and Baz getting it? Or did the man guess the truth and was trying to forestall Damian being charged as an accessory to the burglary! After all, Damian had led the police to the money so maybe the inspector was turning a blind eye. Either way, Damian decided that to say nothing was the best policy. He smiled weakly and nodded in agreement. Minutes later the three policemen left with the stolen money, sand-filled shoes, and some final wisecracks from the crowd.

'Just look at it!' moaned Graham, 'It'll take us hours to rebuild it. Why couldn't it have been the first sandbag?'

'Now who's showing his age?' mocked Tim, keen to get his own back on Graham. 'Too weak and old to dig a little bit of sand,' he taunted. Then he threw back his head and roared with laughter. 'I wouldn't have missed that sight for anything,' he said between guffaws. 'Three policemen digging sand on the beach just like children!' And within seconds, first Graham, then Liz, Damian and the whole of the team were collapsed in helpless fits of laughter at what they had just witnessed. After the tension of the last few days, it was just what they all needed.

It was a very happy team which completed the rebuilding of the pulpit with the help of many of the children who had come along for the afternoon's activities. While Liz and Lydia were putting the artistic finishing touches to the sand, Jenny drew Graham on one side.

'I just wanted to apologise, Graham,' she said. 'I wasn't at all sympathetic to you at first when this all blew up. I even thought you might have done it. I hope you'll forgive me.'

'Yes, of course, Jenny,' said Graham warmly. 'And thanks for saying that. It couldn't have been easy.'

'Well, I know I was a bit of a drain on you all to begin with. But God's really been speaking to me these past couple of days and I want to make a new beginning and put Jesus number one in my life.'

Jenny wasn't the only one exchanging confidences that afternoon. Damian took the opportunity to have a quiet word with Tim.

'I've been thinking,' he began, 'about all those talks I've been hearing.'

'Which talks, Damian?' said Tim, giving him his full attention.

'You know, the ones about money. That woman yesterday said that if you live for money then God wants nothing to do with you.'

Tim smiled at Damian's interpretation of the message but encouraged him to continue.

'Well, it's just that I think I've been like that, you see. I've only really lived from one wage packet to the next, with a few laughs and thrills in between. I suppose that means God's got no time for me.'

'You couldn't be more wrong, Damian. God's got all the time for you you need. All you've got to do is ask.'

'You mean that I could actually know God, sort of have him as part of my life?' said Damian, astonished at how simple Tim had made it sound.

'Yes, that's right,' said Tim. 'Look, why don't we talk some more – say tonight. I could meet you at K Club –

that's if you're still interested.'

'Yeah. OK,' said Damian with enthusiasm. They grinned at each other. Then Graham broke in on them.

'Come on, you two. You must come and see what Liz has done.' He led them impatiently back to the pulpit where Liz and Jenny met them with a broad grin.

'It's in your honour, Damian,' Liz joked, 'so I hope you approve.' She linked arms with him and all four turned to see what she had written in the sand, which had already sent most of the team into stitches again. The words read simply, 'Aren't our policemen wonderful!'

Tim guffawed loudly, then exclaimed, 'But you can't leave that here on the beach for everyone to see! Inspector Martin will have a fit.'

'Don't worry, Tim,' grinned Liz. 'It's only our little joke. I'm sure Lydia will write a more appropriate message for you if you can think of one. Meanwhile, I'd love an ice cream, Damian.'

'Right you are,' laughed Damian. 'Anyone else coming?'

'Yes, we are!' chorused Graham and Jenny. Linking arms they all tripped off to the refreshment kiosk, leaving Tim to explain the pulpit message to some amused passers-by.